I0739120

Dusty and the Cowboy

Coming Home

Dusty and the Cowboy

Coming Home

T. W. Lawrence

Study Guide by
Bryan Tyson

Copyright © 2015 by T. W. Lawrence

All rights reserved. No part of this document may be produced or transmitted in any form, or by any means, electronic or mechanical, including photocopying, recording, or by any information storage and retrieval system without written permission of T.W. Lawrence.

Published by Luckenbach Press

First Printing
Study Guide Edition

ISBN: 978-0-9889605-9-6

DISCLAIMER: This is a work of fiction. Name, characters, places, and incidents are either the product of the author's imagination or are used fictitiously, and any resemblance to actual persons, living or dead; events; or locales is entirely coincidental.

Dedication

This anthology is dedicated to all those who trudge on their personal journey; some days battered, some days praised, but never quitting the trail.

Acknowledgments

If I've learned nothing else in these last few months, it's that writing a book is not something done alone.

I would like to express my heartfelt appreciation for those who helped make me look so good on paper:

My editor: **Fran Lawrence**
My cover artist: **Vanessa Lowry**
My production coordinator: **Roselyn Waiyaki**
My publisher: **Luckenbach Press**

Special thanks to Michael Belk for his great photo used on the front cover. To see more of his work and the path he is now taking, please visit:

www.journeyswiththemessiah.com.

Thank you all,
T.W. Lawrence

Table of Contents

Foreword xiii

All That Glitters 1

Any Horse in Texas 27

Adam's Missing Rib 47

Remember No More 69

Nonesuch 91

Epilogue 123

Call to Action 127

Dusty's Song 129

About Cowboy Church 131

Team Dusty 133

Foreword

I have eagerly awaited the publication of *Coming Home*, the final book in the *Dusty and the Cowboy* trilogy. I have successfully used the first two books, *Lord Show Me the Way* and *Rendezvous*, in our outreach ministry with Cowboys For Christ. *Lord Show Me the Way* is a great tool to use for the person that has not yet had an experience with Christ. The stories in book two, *Rendezvous*, show how Cowboy, the main character, came to know Christ for himself. *Coming Home* will help all of us to reflect on our Christian journey after meeting Christ, whether that be for a day or for decades.

I met the author, T.W. Lawrence, at a cowboy gathering, while I was manning a tent for Cowboys for Christ. This was about the time he released the first book in his trilogy. It became clear that we shared the same passion to reach the lost for Jesus Christ and to encourage people in their Christian walk. Being a cowboy at heart, Cowboys for Christ has given me that opportunity by becoming a Cowboy Chaplain. T.W. shared with me that his goal was not to sell books, but to use the *Dusty and the Cowboy* trilogy for the building and strengthening of the Kingdom of God.

T.W.'s idea to reach the lost, as well as the believer, by using short books of cowboy Christian Historical Fiction, written in easy-to-read prose, clearly works. Each book is organized in chapters, each of which tells a story that compliments the theme of the book. The study questions at the end of each chapter are very useful for individual or group study. I know of several people using these books in Sunday school and for men's Bible study. T.W.'s books are easy to pick up and put down, and they will appeal to those who would not normally read a novel.

T.W., being a native Texan and the son of a veterinarian, uses his background and experiences to make these stories come alive. His characters are believable, and his descriptions vivid, and his facts accurate. T.W.'s research is apparent, and his personal faith and walk with Christ come through in his writing.

Dusty and the Cowboy conveys the message of salvation and living the Christian life without being preachy. I have yet to share one of these books without a request for the next in the series. I am confident you as the reader will not be disappointed. The saying that no hour spent in the saddle is an hour wasted could also be applied to these books. Just sit back and enjoy a good read.

God Bless!

Bob Perkerson

Cowboy Chaplain
Cowboys for Christ

Cattle Trails

All That Glitters

Pi-a-wa-oo, the Comanche call them. They might travel in pairs, but the mountain lion always hunts alone. Seldom seen, these quiet predators fell their prey with deadly leaps from boulder tops or drops from leafy trees. A cougar's print is unmistakable: tear-shaped toes, one front digit extending past the other. No trace of claw. And, the heavy three-lobed heel leaves a distinct impression. Unlike any man on the run, a mountain lion never tries to cover its tracks.

Looking down now at the deep footmarks pressed in muddy snow next to the trail, Cowboy wondered why the big cat had made its way this close to the caprock of the *Llano Estacado*, that palisaded plain of the Texas Panhandle. From where he sat saddle on Dusty, it still required more than three weeks ride, in good weather, to reach this critter's Trans Pecos hunting grounds. Down there, plentiful deer and countless "skunk pigs" roam the rough terrain, providing ample food supply.

It didn't take a tracker's eye to see the panther's path meandered east a bit before disappearing behind some slight rise, now topped with vestiges of melting snow. Before long, if the ache in Cowboy's broken knuckle gave any foretelling, the black-and-purple sky behind him held another of the season's Blue Northers. Darkness stretched the whole length of the rugged escarpment over his shoulder, covering most of the horizon. The storm rushed to dump heavy rain, wet snow, or both along the wrangler's path. That same small rise he gazed upon likely would be buried in the process.

"Glad we quit the high table-lands, Dusty," he said to the buckskin. "Hardly what I'd call habitable. Nary a tree or bush, nor much in the way of water. 'Cepting the occasional seep or a *pozo* at the bottom of some coulee. And too few springs to count." Cowboy looked back for a moment the way they had come. "Animals shun it for good reason," he continued. "Even the tribes crossed there in only two or three special places." The rider pulled the range coat collar tighter against unceasing wind blowing cold against his back. "It's so flat, doubtful you could hear a single echo in that whole expanse between the Canadian River and the Colorado."

Cowboy reined Dusty to a stop when he saw the thin wisp of smoke eking from a broken chimney. Tucked to the wall at the canyon's opening, a dog-run cabin anchored a shabby homestead. Beside it, a barn of no great size stood, attached to a small corral of somewhat questionable construction.

Through the slats in the mesquite fence, six pairs of narrowed eyes watched the horse and rider approach. Instead of searching for more food scraps in the clapboard trough or spending time rooting through the corral's loose dirt, the young hogs huddled tightly in the farthest corner. All heads faced outward, as if this afforded them considerable more protection.

"These swine is more than a mite skittish," Cowboy said to the back of Dusty's ears. Stepping down from the saddle, the rider paused to look at the porkers more closely.

"Wonder if them paw prints is what got 'em so spooked out here in the middle of big lonesome?"

Before Cowboy could begin to speculate on that, a voice called out from the breezeway of the cabin, "What do *you* want?"

The tone clearly matched the unwelcoming look on the woman's face. Standing in the corridor centered atwixt the two lodging compartments, a small figure stood with one hand balled on the hip and the other held to her eyes shading them against the wind and blowing bits of dust. A double-hammer Colt shotgun leaned against the cabin wall next to her feet. Cowboy noticed that both hammers were already cocked.

The wrangler removed his hat as he led Dusty the few steps it took to reach the porch. "Afternoon, miss," he said, looking into her all-but-glaring eyes. "I mean you no harm. I'm just a lone *baccaro* headed…"

He didn't get to finish.

The woman cut him off without warning, "It's missus to you." The scowl boring down at him looked out of place coming from eyes the color of good whiskey. It did little to remove doubt as to her exact wedded status in the midst of this open territory.

"Beg pardon, ma'am," he said with guarded warmth. Cowboy replaced the big hat on his head. "I intend no bother to you or yours. Just a horse and rider headed south to Atascosa County for the spring."

He jerked a thumb over his shoulder at the darkened sky, but kept his eye on her and the loaded scattergun. "Big gust front's comin'. I'd be much obliged just to bed down in your barn 'til this blizzard blows itself out tonight."

He half-turned to assay that tiny structure's actual capacity hold both him and the horse together. Satisfied, he set his attention on the woman once more.

In Cowboy's experience, he found it an easier chore to judge the worth of an unknown *cayuse* than to figure a woman at first meeting. This one certainly would take more than a single glance. He already reckoned by her abrupt manner that she had not been raised in Texas. The woman spoke her words with an accent sounding Southern in origin, but clipped from living in a grand city somewhere. That made the rarity of her unmistakable beauty even more unexpected out here on this isolated homestead.

Cowboy guessed her no more than five feet tall when barefoot. A Cupid's bow mouth enclosed lips neither full nor thin. Her constant biting the lower one made it hard for him to tell. A waist no more than a hand's breadth, down to which hung the ponytail of sleek black hair. The skin's smooth pallor evidenced little exposure to harsh sun. Cowboy judged her certainly no clodhopper's wife, but a most handsome woman just the same.

"What is it, Prudence?" The man's rich baritone did not match his skinny frame as he stepped up behind her. He stood head and shoulders taller than she. Cowboy's eyes were at once drawn to the bulky wrapping of burlap that extended from elbow to knuckles on his right arm. Thin twine, loosely knotted, barely held the sacking in place.

"This man's likely here to steal one of our pigs, Isaac." the woman said. "He certainly looks hungry enough." She held up the shotgun for her husband to take. "Shoot him now, and be done with it."

Isaac shook his head at her while laughing quietly. "You know we can't do that. Not the neighborly thing to do in these parts. Besides, can't be sure I could handle this coach gun with just the one hand." He cast a weak smile in Cowboy's direction, embarrassment touching his jaw. Holding up his unencumbered good palm, Isaac assured the wrangler. "I'm not even left-handed."

"I swear to you, Isaac Coverdale," she said in a quick huff. "Sometimes you are a lean-witted hempseed." Through clenched teeth, Prudence hissed out a long breath that ended in resignation. "Why not just tell this tall stranger that you haven't the means to protect yourself—or me—on this rundown excuse of a farmstead." Prudence propped the gun back against the rough wall. "I did not follow you," she said, "all the way out here from Memphis to die of pneumonia in some drafty cabin. I care not that it belonged to your family."

The sound of her stomping away reverberated in that tiny hallway, punctuated by the creaking of hinges and the crash of wood on wood as the door slammed shut. Both men stared at the cracked flimsy jambs, just waiting for each to crumble from that hard smashing.

"You'll have to forgive her, but my wife has been most poorly of late," Isaac said. "I'm afraid the long journey out here, only to find these conditions…," His good hand swept the breadth of the tiny homestead. "It fairly well broke what was left of her spirit."

Cowboy noted the mix of surrender and regret in the thin man's eyes as the homesteader now studied rough planking at his feet. But the wrangler also recognized a streak of determination beginning to stretch across the other man's features. In all, Cowboy judged him to be a tough hombre; at the moment, standing on the short side of bad luck.

"How'd you come to these parts?" Cowboy asked. "It's a far piece just from here to Redwater, near the shoals you ford the river into Arkansas. And a whole mite further to reach the actual Mississip'."

Isaac began to nurse the bundled arm with fingers of his free hand. He winced with the first touch, and grimaced at the second. "It began with her cousin, Charlie, the sailor. He was down on the ships near the Isle of Cuba. Came home by way of New Orleans." The man looked off to nothing in particular in the near distance. "The Federals panicked over yellow fever coming out of Havana and Santiago. Blockaded the Mississippi north to protect towns along the river." Isaac sat on the stoop, gently resting the bad arm on his knees. "Young Charlie jumped ship and made his way back to Memphis overland. He didn't look that sick when he got home; but folks that could, fled the city when they heard he was there. Including us, after he died."

Cowboy stepped up almost knee to knee with Isaac. "That ain't no dogfall. What calamity has happened here?" He asked, pointing down at the burlap and string.

"This is Providence's way of telling me that I should have remained a gentlemen's banker," Isaac said. "I can no longer cling to the notion that mere visits to a farm as a youth are the same as growing up there." His voice rose to be heard above the freshening wind. It blew harder, carrying with it the smell of impending rain. Isaac could tell that the tall stranger in the broad hat had not gathered the meaning of his words.

"Every spring and summer," the thin man continued, "the family would visit Uncle Harold's one-hundred-and-sixty acres near Robinsonville on the Arkansas side. My two sisters and I would help out with the milking and feeding, alongside our cousins." Cowboy could see that the man had much fondness for this memory. "Uncle would take us boys hunting for one thing or another. We always came home with meat for the pot." Isaac grinned as if that would explain everything. "Why, once or twice I even helped my Uncle make repair to some of the farm buildings. That included applying fresh plaster between the planks of the old smoke house. Much like I was attempting to do here."

Isaac pointed with a long finger to the cabin's logs near the roof. Along the top two rows where dried mortar should have been, only a darkened emptiness remained. Cowboy nodded at the sight, but the other man only shook his head. "I don't understand the thinking here," Isaac said in genuine puzzlement. "Why leave them open all this time when the cabin was finished years ago?"

Cowboy held back his laugh, but he did blurt out a quick breath. "You was too late to summer here," he said. "These mesquite shanties can warm up like a Dutch oven under the hot Texas sun. Homesteaders chip out them spaces for airing heat and patch it back in time for the chinking season of late fall." The wrangler grinned barely half a smile. "You just started considerable late, is all. That how you got the arm?"

Before Isaac could answer, large flakes of wet slush began to pelt both men. Wind blew strong enough to start a faint whine in the distance. The pitch only increased as gusts roared up the canyon past the cabin. Isaac rose, careful not to jostle his wrapped arm.

"Setting out the tools needed to begin this patch work, I fell backwards over a water bucket only to land on a ditching spade handle. A very stout handle, mind you. This is the result." He raised the bad arm. "Broke it, I think. Hurts like the Dickens."

Squinting eyes almost shut, Isaac turned to face west. He said, "Light's almost gone and the weather is upon us. Take your shelter there in the barn, such as it is." He shook his head at the thought. "It should do to keep the wind off you, but not much else. We'll talk more tomorrow." He turned to walk through the same doorway his wife had slammed that short while before.

Cowboy nodded his thanks. Taking Dusty by the reins, he led the buckskin into the tiny structure. Clearly, the wrangler heard no offer of a hot meal. Neither had he been given the excuse for not doing so. Plain bad manners. Feeding strangers, even meagerly, was a long-held tradition on the range. In his heart, Cowboy knew that he likely carried more food in his saddle bags than the Coverdales had in their cabin's larder. He pondered how he should treat that situation come morning. The storm would have blown itself out by then.

***

The sun had yet to fully clear the canyon wall. It sparkled off what few flakes that still clung to the cabin roof. The moaning wind had persisted deep into the night, long after it had dumped the brief but heavy snow. Slush stood pushed up against the windward side of cabin and barn. It piled as high as Cowboy's knees. Now, a steady mildness set in as calm covered the open land. Any wind still moving felt less than a breeze on the wrangler's face.

Cowboy walked with careful strides through the mud as he steered Dusty past the corner of the tiny barn. He held bridle leathers in one hand, his rifle in the other. It surprised him to find Isaac in a somewhat formal coat, long and pitch black in color as the night before had been. The man sat on a worn wooden crate just outside the barn's door. He had both elbows resting on thighs, the good arm raised to cradle his face deep in a narrow palm. Cowboy thought it a pitiful sight.

Isaac started at the appearance of stranger and horse. In a split second his face eased off desperation to show relief. "I…I…" was all he mustered before pushing himself off the box.

"Thought I'd hightailed it out of here without so much as paying my respects?" Cowboy laughed. "You don't know my Ma and how me and my brothers was brought up. Manners is most important back in Atascosa." The wrangler looked at the other man's attire more closely, wondering whether they considered these actual farm duds in Mississippi. "You're a mite dressed up to help me skin this deer."

At those words, Isaac noticed Dusty's burden for the first time. In place of the bedroll and that small extra saddle the buckskin usually carried, the carcass of a large male deer lay strapped across the rump. Its long white tail rested unmoving atop the nearest saddlebag. Examining it more closely, the man could see only the tips of antlers pointing away from him on the other side. He saw, too, that thin mist clinging to its tawny hide as the last escaping warmth met cool morning's air.

"When I spoke of hunting to you last evening," Isaac said in halting tones. "I might not have told that part where only Uncle Harold himself dressed and processed all the meat." The man swallowed hard once, lost some coloring in his cheeks, but could not bring himself to look away.

"Ain't no never mind," Cowboy replied. He led his big horse closer to the barn's door. Over his shoulder, he confided to Isaac, "I just got this pure hankering for some tasty *barbacoa*, meat slow seared over hot mesquite coals. I'd seen fresh deer tracks along the mouth of the canyon afore the storm blew in. Figured they'd hunker down and wait the weather out just like me and Dusty." The wrangler pointed in the direction of far-off brush tops. "They was only a mile or so down the way."

Isaac watched from a safe distance as Cowboy tossed his lariat over a low barn rafter. In a minute, the tall cowman maneuvered Dusty into position and used the rope to suspend the deer. Held tight by the hind hooves, it hung a good foot or so off the dirt floor.

"I calculate that mostly you're a city boy," Cowboy began. "Seems like it or not, circumstance has fated you of late to become a plow chaser." The wrangler swung his head in a slow circle. "Don't see much crops or silage set aside anywheres. Them swine must account for most of your actual food stuffs." Cowboy squinted in the direction of the still-huddled pigs. "I don't figure you for a man who can cut up a hog with much ease, let alone render any lards." He turned back to level his gaze at the thin man. A deep stillness filled the gap between them. The cowboy's face took on a look that bent between quietude and menace. "But for the sake of you and your woman, it's a skill that means survival out here. *Sabe*?"

Isaac stared for a full second before nodding, but he spoke no words. Cowboy's lips softened into a quick smile, but his eyes held little mirth. "Just keep an eye on what I do. You got six chances out there in the pen to get it right." He drew the long blade from its sheath on his belt. "I expect as the missus might fancy some stew meat and shank steaks for fixin's. We best get after it."

Cowboy ran a light thumb along the knife's edge. He frowned a bit, then allowed himself to grin showing full teeth. "Besides," he said. "Possible it will take a spell longer to sharpen this old *chuchillo* here than to do the actual skinning."

It did.

It also took some time to crumble up salt lumps found in a tight-lidded clay jar. That stout pottery squatted in a corner of the barn until Cowboy moved it to lay out his bedroll. He showed Isaac how to rub the seasoning vigorously top and bottom onto the meat just cut. "You're going to need," the wrangler said, "to cut these gunny sacks to strips. Then wrap 'em tight around each chunk of venison." While the man did so, Cowboy drug the crate into the barn and began packing meat bundles inside the box. "This'll keep vermin and such from being tempted," he said.

Isaac hustled about to complete the chore. On the man's face Cowboy could see the faintness of a childlike joy. In his mind, the younger man must be reliving Uncle Harold's farm visits or maybe he was just grateful not to face certain starvation. When Isaac finished packing the crate, Cowboy said, "It's a nuisance we ran out of salt. Get you some store-bought in town, and cure what meat's left she don't cook up right away. This weather, it should keep you to the end of spring."

The first dark cloud of the morning passed over Isaac's face. "I'm not certain the folks at the general store will accommodate that," he said. "We're well in debt to them as it is. Mr. Kessler advanced us the purchase of the twelve pigs two months ago. Plus he obliged us these few provisions we've been living off of." His voice trailed down to a near whisper as he finished.

Cowboy knew a confession like that, for someone of his once lofty position, could bash the man's pride completely. "Living on the tick," the wrangler said, "is a darn tough row to hoe. Done so myself in younger days, vexing 'til I got out from under." For no apparent reason that Isaac could see, Cowboy nodded to himself. The puncher had made a decision to that unsettled quandary rolling over and again in the back of his mind. To the other man he simply said, "It's near mid-morning and I'm settin' out at first light. We best get to chinking them logs, if we're to get you any relief from that wind."

***

The sun hung halfway to dusk by the time the two men stopped to move chinking gear to a new spot. That assortment consisted of a bucket holding remnants of clay dug from the hillside, broken dried twigs, and melted snow; the ditching spade; and a wooden churn Cowboy stood on to reach high spots on the open logs.

Admiring their labor thus far, Cowboy swept his hand in the direction of the finished wall. "My Ma would tell us long about now, 'Boys, it's a thing of *purty*.'" Isaac had to agree, proud of the work even if he only sloshed the bucket contents around one-handed with the broad shovel. "To my recollection," Cowboy said, "You ain't spoke of how come you by this place? Belong to your kin?"

Before answering that question, the thin man made certain that his wife had not returned with the last bit of clay from the hill. "My folks live in Bald Knob, not that far from my uncle in Robinsonville." he said. "They welcomed us as always and were happy to put us up until the fever scare played out." His gaze shifted toward the approaching woman now struggling to carry her small pail. "That is, they did until they heard how we looked after Charlie until he gave up the ghost. After a spate of shouts and accusations, my father gave us a handful of hard money in a kerchief and the reins to a swayback old nag pulling that whiskey shay over there." Isaac appeared reconciled to this circumstance. "The last thing he did was give me the papers to this place, with the hope that we would not die disheartened out here the way his step-mother had done."

"But mostly, he wanted us gone," Prudence called out from the length of about ten paces. Even at that distance and her husband's low tones, she knew the substance of his words. "That sorry horse died just short of Texarkana," she said. "Bought another one and spent the rest of our money getting here." Prudence handed the pail to Cowboy. Her eyes, less fierce than before, did not leave his face. Finding no answers there, she pulled her shawl tighter and turned to let the sun warm her back.

"I figure it's done in an hour's time," Cowboy said. He helped Isaac mix the final batch of mortar before heaving himself up on the churn once more. The wrangler dolloped plaster into the length of decreasing open space with quick strokes of his makeshift ladle. When all had been filled he stepped down. "This time three days from now, that'll all be dried hard as any caliche slag."

Cowboy found himself facing Prudence eye-to-eye now after she stepped up on the porch. "Why have you done all this?" she asked. Interest rather than scorn held her look this time. "You provided us with sustenance enough to last us through the winter. Now you've kept us from freezing as well. You showed us where to find deadfall firewood down in the canyon and a spring with better water than in our old well." Her eyes moistened slightly, but not quite to tears.

"Weren't much when you think about it, ma'am," the wrangler said. "Raised as I was in Atascosa, this is all in a day's chores for us four brothers."

He turned to help Isaac, already busy cleaning up the clutter. He turned back when Prudence spoke again, "You demand nothing from us in return. Neither have you taken advantage of a crippled man, or his wife." She bent an inch or two toward the wrangler. "There must be *something* that you want."

Cowboy slid the Stetson from his head. "For a fact, ma'am," he said, "there is. Before I take Dusty and ride down the trail," the big man paused, "just once before I go," he paused a second time to affix his most somber look, "I'd like to see you smile."

Caught so unawares by that request, the corners of Prudence's mouth twitched at once. While not a true smile, her face held a mild delight. Isaac could barely hold back his own tears at a sight not seen since Memphis. "Sir," she said to the wrangler, "I will gladly grin like a possum for you. Moreover, I will dance at your wedding, but first please rid us of that cussed catamount savaging our pigs." She softened her eyes in hopeful supplication. "Half of them are gone now. Soon, we'll have nothing to sell in the market next spring."

Cowboy swung around to survey the remaining swine, then looked back at the man, and last at his wife. He grinned now, more smirk than mirth. "I truly 'spect that big cat won't bother you no more."

***

The cougar stopped when he smelled the blood. In another moment, the cat found a heap of deer guts left at the base of the tree. That double mouthful, he gobbled down in big bites as though famished. The light of this night's full moon glimmered off the snow in a brilliant sparkle. That illuminated the feline's fur with a dazzling glow. It outlined the shape of the cat's body unmistakably in the clear night's air.

For a long minute, a rough tongue licked mouth and chin to taste the last of the unexpected morsel. The panther's ever-moving nostrils searched more scent, and found something of interest nearby. This time, it drifted down from a fixed spot between the low-hung limbs.

At a height of about eight feet, remnants of the deer's ribs and part of its skull leaned against the tree's bark, tacked there by a hand-forged nail. Unsatisfied hunger, mixed with curiosity, made the cougar raise up on hind legs to sniff at this next helping of easy food just barely within its extended paw's reach.

Next to the barn, Cowboy used the corral's top rail to balance the Winchester. He steadied the sight on a spot at the base of the skull, between and just below the cat's cocked ears. The wrangler eased out his breath until it was gone. He could feel the curve of the trigger hug the tip of his finger.

At this distance it would be hard to miss.

***

Even if a man can step across it in a single stride, Texans will call it a river. They're just proud to have water running through the countryside. So it was in Cooperville. Cowboy watched the thin trickle eke its way along the ditch to form the settlement's northern perimeter. He hoped the melting snow would eventually give it an actual torrent someday.

The wrangler rode the big horse into town. A fresh set of cougar's claws, wrapped tight in muslin scraps, lay snugged in the over-stuffed saddle bags. In a quick scan, Cowboy noted the five wooden structures that comprised the mercantile establishments; four of them two-story. Not a saloon to be found among them. That seemed surprising to him for a county seat and the only established community for many miles around.

Just past the Wayfarers Hotel, an imposing whitewashed lodging with its wide porch wrapped around the second floor, sat a low, squat, but wide building. The narrow walkway there exhibited a series of tall posts supporting a gabled wooden canopy. Above that, unmistakable bold red lettering proclaimed the words, "Kessler Lumber Company—General Merchandise—Market—Post Office." An old man sat alone in a stiff chair outside the double-door entryway. He watched Cowboy and Dusty approach but appraised neither horse nor rider with his scrutiny. Instead, he fixed his look on the fancy extra saddle tied on the buckskin's rump. The man took note of the matching bridle also fixed along there.

"Hold up there, friend," the older man said to Cowboy. "How come you by that fancy rigging? A bit showy for a working hand."

"For a fact," Cowboy said, "it is." With those few words he let his face go blank, expecting the old man possibly to launch into some serious barter. "I got this for helping a fella up the way find a good outfit for his pony. He couldn't ride no more."

"That right?" the man asked. After a long pause, he continued, "Name's Kessler. My emporium here." He indicated his name painted on the window with a thumb. "Don't much see the likes of that seat, skirt, or strings in these parts. Not seem to suit you or the horse, if you don't mind my saying." He stared up at the tall rider's eyes, but could read little in them. "Care to parley a trade?"

"What's the offer?"

"You get down to it, don't you?"

Cowboy just stared in reply.

"I'll give you forty dollars for the both of them; silver coin or federal paper."

"That's a start," Cowboy said, almost without moving his lips.

"Don't sour my milk, son; I intend to have those leathers!" Kessler stood now to point at the rig. "We can dicker 'til sundown, and I won't budge above fifty. But I will throw in a dinner over at the wife's cafe. Feed you 'til you're full as a tick: Beefsteak, home fries, biscuits, and my Martha's apple pie. Some grains for the horse, too, if you'll walk him over to the livery."

Cowboy stepped off Dusty to stand in the dirt at the store's sidewalk. He stood face-to-face with the old man and took his hand. "I can set with that, Mr. Kessler," he said. "A duck-on-a-rock if it ain't a fair deal. Saddle's yours, bridle too." The wrangler began to unhitch the rig from his mount.

"Come inside," Kessler said. "We'll settle up."

A low wooden counter ran the length of one wall; its rough milled lumber now rubbed smooth by years of wear. From beneath it, Kessler retrieved an angular metal box stacked atop a cloth-bound journal. Plentiful lined-paper sheets stuck out from its covers. Out of the box the old man counted out the purchase price: twenty-five silver dollars, twenty-five in paper currency. Before shoving the money across the counter to Cowboy, Kessler wet a pencil's tip with his tongue then wrote figures and notes in the journal.

"Big as your mercantile is," Cowboy said, "I'll wager half the county has a page in that tally book of yours."

"In that you would be wrong, stranger." Kessler patted the pages with unbending fingers. "I got the *whole* county in here," he smiled with enormous satisfaction.

"That include them new corn-knockers I met at the canyon mouth about ten miles back? Pretty woman with a slim-as-could-be husband?"

"Ah yes, the Coverdales." Kessler's face clouded at the mere sound of the name. "I told Martha that those two could not cut it out here. Said that lending money to them was a fool's errand." He shook his head at the memory. "But my wife would have none of it. So, those two are down on the page for dry goods, supplies, a dozen pigs, and some feed. I'm letting them raise the herd to market size." In near dejection, the old man flipped the sheets until he got to the Coverdale page. "Doubtful I'll see any of it, but they owe eighteen dollars. And that's with the pigs at a better than fair price."

Cowboy took the two top coins off one the five stacks. Those he put in a coat pocket along with the pile of paper money. The remaining silver dollars he pushed back to a shocked Kessler. "That should square the account and leave them five to the good," the wrangler said.

Looking at the unasked, but obvious question in the old man's face, Cowboy said, "I can't make up for the misfortune that's followed them up 'til now. But I can, at least, stake them to a fightin' chance." Nodding to himself more than Kessler, he finished, "They did me a good turn is all."

Cowboy tipped his hat to the still speechless store owner. "Reckon the café's in the hotel, next building over?" the old man nodded an imperceptible reply as the wrangler left him to stew in his wonderment.

***

It didn't take long to get Dusty started on his helping of feed at the stable. It took Cowboy even less to settle himself at a small table in the somewhat rustic dining room. The Sharps Big Fifty leaned against the wall behind him, next to the Winchester 73. Cowboy's saddlebags draped over the back of the closest chair. From one, both boxes of .50 cal shells sat table top within his reach, almost touching the half-filled coffee cup. An empty china plate held nothing more than gristle and a chunk of bone. He'd left the merest scrap of potato untouched, while the apple pie was completely gone. Only the hanging scent of cinnamon remained.

Cowboy ran two fingers idly along the top and sides of each corrugated box, staring but not seeing the fancy logo printed there. His mindless contemplation stopped when he looked up to the tear-stained face of Prudence Coverdale. "Mr. Kessler said I'd find you here," she said. "Isaac finally came to see Doc McKay about his arm. I went to the store instead to beg more supplies, salt and such. I thought I could buy more time to pay back with this." In her extended palm she held a dented silver dollar. "I saw you slip it into Isaac's coat while he was mixing plaster," she went on. "I took it and never told him anything. I didn't want him to be the one that came to Kessler groveling." Her tears flowed again in great profusion. "I've done you grievously."

Cowboy stood at once. The napkin stayed tucked beneath his chin and spread across his chest. He pulled a chair for her to sit. "Ma'am. There's no need," he began.

"From the beginning," Prudence said, "I have treated you with sniping and distain. I poured anger on you meant for others. I even asked to have you shot." She pulled out an embroidered hanky from a sleeve. With that, she dabbed her face, collecting the tears and deep regrets that lingered there. "You have responded to all this with helpfulness and acts of kindness. I feel so very much ashamed."

"Might not have spoke on it, Miz Coverdale," Cowboy said after a moment, "but I was reared in a God-fearing home. Each night after supper Ma or Pa would read us Scripture, to school us in those mindful ways."

She nodded with a knowing look. "There was an old Bible left in the cabin when we got there," Prudence said. "I have been reading it for some needed comfort. One of the Psalms says, 'I will lift up mine eyes unto the hills, from whence cometh my help. My help cometh from the Lord, which made heaven and earth.' My prayer was that such help be given us." She looked down at the hands in her lap. "Unfortunately, I was too blinded by my anger to consider that what *was* sent—was you."

He grinned with reassurance. "Lending a hand back there was the rightly thing to do."

"What about the money you put up at Kessler's store?" she asked. "I can't say when that ever will be repaid."

Cowboy held up a broad hand. "Truth is, I was gifted with that saddle by circumstance back up the trail. Fair to say it was heaven sent. Sharing that just makes my heart go easy." His ready smile made her heart feel lighter. "If what I done gets you and Isaac off to a fair start, then I'm paid-in-full. Texas can use good folks like you."

Prudence rose to her feet once more. She took the time to straighten out her dress and coat. The moistened kerchief got tucked back into the cuff. "I have trouble expressing gratitude. I must confess I don't know why that is."

"Well, ma'am," Cowboy said. "I'm told it starts when we realize that nothing in this world gets done by the strength of ourselves alone."

"Then, thank you for the gift of deer and cougar pelts. That covering will keep us warm at night and give us peaceful sleep. God bless you, 'lone *baccaro*'."

She squeezed his big hand with both of hers. A look of warmth and budding encouragement replaced the former desolation. Prudence let go with obvious reluctance, turned without further word, and left Cowboy standing alone in the dining room.

***

Fed, watered, and saddled, the big horse was ready. Cowboy looked again into the heavier of the two cartridge boxes he'd gotten from the preacher weeks before, along with the Sharps rifle. Four huge gold nuggets were all that he could see. "It's doubtful," he said to Dusty, "Brother Van knew that dead prospector found treasure in the mountains after all."

The wrangler shrugged. Finally, he accepted that this gift was meant to be his. "I reckon them pieces is enough to buy back Pa's ranch from that chintzy banker. Takes some of the sting out of going home." Cowboy heaved himself into the saddle. With the press of a single knee, he turned his mount south toward Atascosa.

They loped the trail at an easy pace.

Their journey had begun.

All That Glitters
Study Questions

1. How is Cowboy's generous gift of canceling the debt without seeking anything in return like God's gift of salvation to us?

2. Why was Cowboy willing to give so much? How did Cowboy knowing the saddle was not his make him willing to be generous?

3. We are all like Prudence, because we have a debt we cannot pay. How is that debt paid?

Any Horse in Texas

Big or small, a cattle outfit is only as good as the horses they ride. It matters not what time of year, the color, or the breed—or even whether you're standing north or south of the river. In Texas, there are only four cow pony temperaments to be found: the jumpy, the good-natured, the loner, or the all-but-unbroken. Cowboy knew this. He also knew that a man cannot teach a horse without being taught in return. The many miles he rode on Dusty begat their friendship. Countless days they spent together forged their trust.

Cowboy believed that with a good horse beneath him and a dependable rifle within reach, he could trek just about anywhere in cattle country to get work done for the brand. His big buckskin was no longer a colt, although Dusty had not been much older when Cowboy chanced to saddle him the first time. Now, the wrangler let this horse—still strong in his gait—lead the way down the trail, familiar or unknown.

For three days they followed the river south until horse and rider came to the old military highway. That worn dirt road extended west as far as El Paso, after crossing over the Pecos. To the east, it made its way to San Antonio. Cowboy turned Dusty now heading toward the Alamo city. At the horizon's edge, bumping up from constant flats that seemed only interrupted by occasional curly mesquite clusters and knots of buffalo grass, the wrangler saw the beginnings of the central hill country. "Dusty," he said, "best to start remembering where it was we last saw Emma. I calculate by sundown tomorrow we'll be close. And we got that promise to keep."

That recollection together with the mild air and bright sunshine brought the cowman much contentment. The mood stayed with him as they veered off the broad throughway to take a lesser road used by freighters and mail coaches to reach the small towns started there by hearty German immigrants. Cowboy recalled these Rhinelanders loved to haggle over every little thing. They deemed no detail insignificant.

The sun had yet to cross the noon meridian when they forded a narrow stream that barely reached Dusty's fetlocks at full depth. Beginning immediately on the opposite shore, an uphill grade began. Steep and more rocky than sand, the road held a tight band of shoulder-high vegetation near its crest. This dense Rabbit Thorn thicket clustered over an acre or more on both sides of their pathway.

As they made their way slowly almost to the top, Cowboy saw that a small clearing opened to his left. He doubted that gap could hold ten small cows or three large longhorns, but his eye was drawn to the commotion unfolding in its midst. By the agonizing cries, the horse sounded in serious pain. The gelding tried in vain to loosen the grip of the man standing on the ground beating him across the withers.

That distinct sound of leather striking flesh stirred Cowboy's anger. He wheeled the buckskin in that direction. Almost without urging, Dusty sprinted toward the bully at full gallop. As they approached, Cowboy could see the cruel assailant to be a young man of eighteen or nineteen years. His hat lay stomped on the ground. One suspender fallen off the shoulder now draped across his elbow.

Neither hearing nor seeing the encroaching horse and rider, the young man dropped the belt from his hand to pick a coiled lariat up from the ground. He seemed single-minded to continue the brutal flogging.

"STOP THAT, you crockhead!" Cowboy yelled, "You got no call to whip an animal like that!" He reined in Dusty with one hand as he leaned out over the saddle. The wrangler caught the rope's loop as it reached the top of its backward arc. He slid quickly to the ground still clinging the lariat. Without too much effort Cowboy won the brief tug-of-war, ending with his complete possession of the rope.

For his part the young man looked neither chastised nor concerned, let alone afraid. He spoke first, "I'ze you, old man, I'd get on my horse and ride away from things that ain't none your business." His eyes betrayed a mild amusement. His body crouched into a dare.

Cowboy calculated that he was not old enough to be this boy's father by any stretch, and second, that he'd seen this hot-headedness many times before. All too often, in those rough-and-tumble supply towns along the trail, some rider from another outfit would spoil loudly for a fight. The reason didn't really matter; neither did the victim.

"Well, I ain't you, *pendejo*," Cowboy said in quiet tones, "'Cuz I know that twenty miles in one direction and forty in the other with no town in sight, is not a place to be crippling my only means of getting there." The wrangler raised the rope buckle high. "Getting lashed with loops of braided hemp hurts like blazes." The lariat swayed slightly in his grip, inviting the shorter man to learn if what Cowboy said was true.

The youngster coughed out a high-pitched snort. "What *you* don't know," he said, "is that I'm Kid Tyson. I could air out your liver with this Schofield 44." His hands hovered over the darkened pistol butt in anticipation.

Cowboy brushed past him without a word, outstretching his arms with palms down, to ease up to the pinto pony now cowering against the juniper hedge. For minutes the wrangler took small steps, spoke gentle tones, and finally placed a hand on the pony's rump, halfway between back and tail. Once he felt the horse relax a bit, Cowboy ran the hand down one back leg and lifted up the hoof for an appraising look.

"See that dark color there? Around that small stone stuck in the groove between the frog and the sole?" Cowboy asked. "Got a bad bruise. He's road sore for sure." Disgust spread across the wrangler's mouth and eyes. His head shook back and forth in disbelief. "Sakes alive, *hombre*, didn't you feel him limping?"

Cowboy had to repeat his last question to get an answer. Rather than take interest in the pinto's condition, Tyson devoted most of his attention instead to the buckskin. He paid careful attention to the rigging, saddle bags, and rifles that the big horse carried.

"I thought he was just coming up lazy," Tyson said, "Cussed him for being so troublesome after we came though that rock field yonder." He nodded off to his left. Not a care seemed evident on his face. "Couldn't keep him to a trot much after that. But we still made good time and nobody saw me come up to this hidey place."

Cowboy approached the pinto once more. He touched the still sticky drying blood oozed from a series of short gashes across the flank near the belly. This damage came from the huge rowels of the boy's spurs, each containing fourteen sharp points. The wrangler turned back to the young rowdy once more. He said, "You call to mind an old pal I rode the cattle trail with many times. He was tough on his horses, but not merciless like you. Name of Frankie Peppers."

"Told you, old man. My name is Kid Tyson."

Cowboy ignored the protest to continue. "He was mixed-blood. His ma came from one of the northern tribes. She was the one taught him how her people view nature and the world."

Tyson eased slightly his posture from obvious provocation to a more mild interest. "What's this to do with my lame horse?" he asked.

"One night over bacon and beans," Cowboy said, "he told us how his ancestors believed that when they looked into the eyes of a horse, they did not just see an animal. Instead they saw another living being. They saw a friend. They felt its soul."

"Yeah, well, I'll tell you what I see." Tyson said, "four hooves, a mane, and a tail. One nag is as good as any another." He dropped down into the crouch again. This time, he drew the Schofield from its holster. That, he leveled at Cowboy's chest. "Me and this buckskin of yours are going to ride together from now on." His lips curled into a grin, that of a wolf about to snarl. "Seeings how both your rifles are strapped to this saddle and you carry no pistols in your belt, I expect you won't put up much fuss." Tyson laughed. "Call it an even trade for the pinto."

The wrangler stood unmoving. He looked first to Dusty, whose ears cocked forward as if he were following the words being spoken, then to Tyson who backed up far enough to grab the reins still draped in a ground tie. "Afore you go to getting in a bad way," Cowboy said, "I must apprise you." He raised one big hand to point directly at Dusty's head. Instead of using just the index finger, the hand extended as though forming a salute. "Dusty's not easy to sit saddle on. In fact, he has a streak of mean."

Undeterred, Tyson responded with a practiced casual boast, "Old man, it's a known fact that I can ride *any* horse in Texas." He threw one rein around the buckskin's neck. With the other in hand, he stuck his boot up at a stirrup. He missed twice as Dusty crabbed a step or two sideways each time he tried. Cussing now, Tyson grabbed the horn and, with seeming ease, swung himself atop the saddle in a single effort.

"Whatever you have in mind," Cowboy said, "one thing you should ought never do…"

The words came too late. Tyson jerked Dusty's head around with a ferocious tug. "I'll show you who's boss," he told the big horse. The rider sunk the spurs of both boots into Dusty's sides. That got the buckskin moving - but not as Tyson intended. From a restless standstill, Dusty bolted like a shot for three long strides. Horse and rider were soon to the opening of the thicket, only a few steps from the roadway. Without so much as a break in rhythm, the buckskin lengthened his gait ever so little. Then he jammed both front hooves into the dirt. His neck bent down so that the jaw now almost grazed the ground.

Unprepared for this unexpected drama and caught with his weight too far forward to recover from the sudden stop, Tyson barrel-rolled heels over hat to land hard on the rocky roadbed. His right shoulder took the brunt of the fall. He didn't bounce much, if at all.

Cowboy came at the run. He hoped to prevent what he feared was coming next, but he was not nearly quick enough.

Dusty reared up slightly; sufficient enough to bring his hooves down hard on the rider's body. Once. Twice. Three times the big horse did this before Cowboy could pull him away.

The wrangler eyeballed Tyson's chest until he could see him breathing. "God ain't through with you yet, pard," Cowboy told the prostrate figure covered in the trail's dirt and dust. "Otherwise you surely would not survive a fall like that." He saw the blood start to drip from the young man's mouth. "Tried to warn you that Dusty don't much cotton to spurs."

Cowboy waited in silence. For minutes, Tyson did not respond beyond taking shallow and increasingly noisy breaths. "You're busted up good," the wrangler said softly. "Can you move at all?"

At last the young rider stirred, rolling his head to one side. With what little wind he could muster, Tyson began to cough out phlegm, saliva, and blood. "It hurts all over. Mostly my shoulder and ribs." he said in halting whispers. He tested his left arm, to find it still useful. Tyson placed a hand on Cowboy's forearm, clutching it more as he found strength. In a voice now no more than a groan, barely to be heard above the afternoon's light breeze, Tyson said, "Please, mister, don't let me die out here alone."

He eyes closed as a stupor overtook him. The young rider left Cowboy alone with only the sounds of raspy wheezing.

***

Stopping for a moment, the wrangler watched dusk fade to encroaching darkness. In the southwest, the evening star dazzled like some bright beacon. Cowboy lamented that this early in the year, its stellar companion no longer paired up for their nightly celestial journey. That other star lay hidden now somewhere below the horizon.

Since Tyson spoke to him last and swooned, Cowboy busied himself with a host of needed tasks. He gently pulled the stone from the pinto's hoof. Then rubbed the wound with the juice of a single chili pepper found abandoned in the bottom of his saddle bag. Something he watched *vaqueros* do time and again on the long cattle drives north. It was said to reduce any swelling. This pony put up no fuss at all.

To give the injury an extra measure of protection, the wrangler wrapped the hoof with small strips cut from Tyson's bedroll blanket. Removing both saddles, Cowboy hobbled the horses outside the juniper hedge. There, they could graze their fill on a tall patch of greening weeds and other rough vegetation. Last, he built a fire to boil coffee. Something needed to wash down the salted venison he chewed with slow precision. Cowboy took the little leather-bound book from the range coat's pocket, leaned on one elbow near the fire, and mumbled the words aloud to more fully grasp their meaning.

From the roadway, Cowboy soon heard a moaning and the rustling of movement. He turned to find Tyson almost sitting. The bad right arm clutched to the chest at an odd angle. Labored breathing came steady but loud. Once the young rider tried to suck in a complete lungful of air. Even in the campfire's dim light Cowboy could see the pain that caused.

"We're gonna need to find you a sawbones, for sure," Cowboy said. "What little doctoring I done in this life was first time I pushed cattle up the trail. Helped the cook tend to drovers' discomfitures, mostly rope burns and other scrapes and bruises." He looked at the sagging heap of flesh and bones that had been a feisty adolescent mere hours before. "Cookie told cowhands busted up bad they had three choices: find a doctor, tend to it theirselves, or die." His face took on a look of encouragement. "Them last two ain't in the cards—yet."

He helped Tyson to his feet with great effort. After a dozen plodding steps he got the young man off of the road and out of more harm's way. Cowboy propped the now quiet young man against a saddle next to the fire. He offered up supper meat but Tyson just shook his head. The boy did take the tin of coffee extended to him. He cradled the cup against his chest below the chin, letting the warmth comfort him some.

Tyson spoke. "I heard you muttering there in the dark," he said. "What is that all about? You that lonesome out here in the wild?"

"Never," Cowboy replied in a quiet but even tone. He held up the small Bible for Tyson to see. "As long as I got the Good Book in my hand and the Lord in my heart, I never ride these trails alone. How about you?"

"I hurt too much to talk church with you. It smarts even to draw breath." Tyson grimaced as he did so. "Reckon the pain will ever quit?" he asked.

"Not likely anytime soon," Cowboy said. "Now stick out that tongue of yours. Loll it over this away." Tyson did so. "Now tuther." The boy did so again. With a keen eye the wrangler saw the dark red knot swelling on one side of the pinkish tissue. It still oozed a bit of blood. "Bit yourself when you hit the ground," Cowboy told him, "That likely accounts for the mouth bleed. Could have been bad otherwise." He cut a juniper sprig from the hedge using his long knife. That he handed to Tyson. "Chomp on this."

Gently the wrangler ran long fingers along the young man's ribs, stopping whenever Tyson flinched or moaned. For several minutes Cowboy repeated this crude examination until satisfied. At last he said, "Seems some is cracked, others is broke. None poking through. That's lucky," He nodded to the boy. "But you need help better than me."

Tyson spit green bits and resin from the tip of his tongue. He tried washing the bad taste out with the remaining Arbuckle coffee but bitterness lingered. "That hedge is no good for eating," he said.

"For a fact, it ain't," Cowboy replied, "but it's a good place to hide. What was you doin' hole up in the junipers? More than just beating a horse."

Tyson shifted from resting on one hip to the other. His eyes did not quite meet Cowboy's. "Guess it don't matter much now," he said. "I was fixing to rob the stagecoach on its way to Mecklenburg. Gonna steal their strongbox full of gold and silver." His eyes still lit up at the thought of it.

Cowboy could not help himself. He laughed from deep in the belly. "Well, Kid Tyson," he said, "How you come to figure on that? We're miles south of where the Oxbow Route carrying the Overland Stage crosses that military highway. Only gold around here gets hauled is by the U.S. Army. And that's on the big road back yonder." The wrangler shook his head in true disbelief. "Last I seen, that Army pay wagon always has a troop of armed cavalry with it." His arm stretched out to point at the dirt track he'd just taken Tyson off of. "That path is too small for a Comstock Coach like the Overland outfit uses." Cowboy said, "Most can travel this path is a farm wagon or that buckboard carrying mail under government contract." He shook his head again in amusement. "Doubtful you'll get rich bushwhacking either of them."

The wrangler stood, grabbing the remainder of Tyson's torn blanket. He began to rip a long strip from the remaining material. All the while Cowboy could see that the boy followed his movements with a mix of wonderment and scrutiny, but Tyson said nothing. With the task finished and the knife back in the sheath, Cowboy rolled the remnant into a tight bunch. He knelt beside Tyson to place one end of the ripped blanket in the midst of the boy's chest.

"On a cattle drive once't out of Nueces," the wrangler said, "we had a cowhand not much older than you, get kicked by a longhorn bad enough to smash some ribs. Ray Patterson was the *segundo* of the outfit back then." Cowboy began to wrap the blanket under Tyson's arms and around his back. "Ray trussed that boy up tight with a length of canvas so the cowhand could breathe without hurting. It oughta work for you."

Minutes passed before the dressing cinched around Tyson's ribcage completely. The wrangler helped the boy stand so as to better judge the effect of his efforts. In a breathy tone, the boy said, "Tell old Ray for me that his cure has some promise. I can draw and exhale without so much hurt."

"Ray's dead," Cowboy replied, "but he woulda been the first to be happy for you. And the first to say you was stupid. A desperado you ain't." Cowboy tucked the tattered end piece under the bandaging. "What in the world possessed you to pick this very spot?" he asked.

Tyson's pride showed in the grin that gripped his face. "Easy enough," the boy said, "the road runs steep next to these junipers, coach is barely moving with all that weight. I get the drop on 'em sudden-like, relieve them of their strong box, and hightail it out of here a richer man."

"Come up with that all by yourself, did you?" Cowboy asked.

"Naw, it was that three-card monte scheme. The one where you bet some sucker that he can't follow the ace of spades when you shuffle just the ace, a ten, and a king on a table top. Like the game of thimblerig, hiding the pea under one of three thimbles." Tyson's grin faded to a face of clear regret. "Turns out I didn't have the hands for it. All thumbs. Ended up, I either lost money paying the suckers when they actually won, or got beat down hard when it was obvious I was trying to put the cheat on them."

"Sounds like you was the actual sucker," the wrangler said.

"Maybe," Tyson replied. He tugged the blanket strip with both hands to better fit his breathing. "Met this man playing billiards for money in a saloon near Kerrville. After three shots of red-eye, he blathered on about how easy it was to hold up a stage. Sheriffs covering too much territory, no money for posses, little interest in chasing robbers outside of their jurisdiction." Tyson eased himself next to the fire once more, taking up the coffee cup again. "He claimed he'd made a fortune robbing stages in California, but he must a spent it cause he sure looked down on his luck when I was there buying liquor for him and listening to him tell me his endless stories."

Cowboy sat opposite the boy, facing east. The darkness now began to fade to that bluish-black that foretells the coming light. He nodded toward hills on the horizon just beginning to be seen in vague silhouette. "Dawn is coming soon," he said. "I reckon you can still ride once we get you on the horse and if we go slow. With the pinto limping like he is, slow is all we got."

"And then what?" Tyson asked. An edginess crept into his voice; the sound of a man down in his boots, not that of defiance.

"I figure we back-trail to the military highway," Cowboy said. "Then head ourselves toward Austin. Long about Fredericksburg, we should come upon Fort Scott."

The wrangler nodded to himself in the gathering light, agreeing with his own plan. "They should have a doctor there could help you out." He tossed remains of cold coffee on the fire's ashes, sending up a brief sizzle of thin smoke.

In a moment, Cowboy stood. He grabbed up his saddle and bridle leathers. "While I'm loading the horses, you should give some thought to changing your life. Keep heading down the trail you're on, and serious bad is bound to befall." He turned to go cinch up Dusty, but turned back when he heard Tyson's whimpering break out to a bawl.

"I'm just no good at anything," the boy said, "not bushwhacking. Not cards. I can't even rob folks with that big pistol of mine without ending up with more trouble than money." The boy wracked himself with blubbering sobs. The stabbing pain to his ribs lay hidden beneath the tears streaming over his cheek. "I'm a faker, too. No one calls me Kid Tyson but me," he confessed. "My real name is Burl Tyson. Baby sister called me Burley, before I run off from home last year. I was no good being a farm hand either. My father said as much." He looked up at the wrangler, eyes wet, confusion dancing there with the agony pouring from his heart. "What am I going to do?"

The wrangler looked down at the crestfallen young man. "You might begin by letting go," he said, "Stop clinging to the thoughts and deeds that bring you pain and ruin. Fall into the arms of the Lord and let him carry you to the destiny that He has planned for you." Cowboy stuck a hand in his range coat. At last, he pulled out the small Bible. That he handed to Tyson.

"You might want to look at the passage from Luke. Start with the twenty-third chapter, long about the forty-second verse. Just hours before he died, the thief on the cross called on the Savior. Even that man's soul was spared the eternal confines of Hell. I find great comfort in that."

Tyson did not take the book when offered to him. His look became even more forlorn. He said, "It's not that I don't appreciate your offer, mister. I can see you are a sincere man of God. It's not even that I truly believe the Lord would have no use for a low down fool like me." The boy swallowed hard without taking his eyes from those of the wrangler's. "Comes down to it, I can't read."

Heart almost breaking from hearing that knowledge, Cowboy squat on boot heels. He turned to the passage indicated and slowly read the Scripture aloud in his soft baritone. The wrangler looked up at each verse ending. Tyson nodded along as he heard each word being spoken. In the distance, the sunrise crested the meager treeless hills. Morning's first rays of light began to touch them both.

***

Tyson lay in the back of the Army wagon, resting on the contraption thrown together by the affable Sergeant Major McIntyre. Half hammock, half wounded man's litter, it swung freely hung by its ropes. McIntyre calculated the boy would rather sway a bit, than to feel each bump along the rock-strewn highway. He draped a stout cavalry blanket up to Tyson's midsection before stepping back down to his horse.

Cowboy shook the hand the Sergeant Major offered him. The Army man said, "It's more than a miracle that you found us out here on this open road. We only muster from the fort for supplies every fourth month." The man adjusted his uniform and tightened leather gauntlets to his wrists. "Your friend is in good hands now," he said, "and we'll see that he mends proper."

"I only come upon the boy a day ago," Cowboy said, "From what little we spoke, I'd say he has the makings to become a good man."

Mounting up, the Sergeant Major looked to Tyson first and then to the wrangler standing in the road next to his horse. "Army's short of volunteers at the moment," he said, "we might even try to recruit him."

McIntyre called orders to his troops, who responded sharply. To the wrangler he shouted over his shoulder, "We'll be late as it is. We must move out. Make your farewells, but please be brief."

Cowboy nodded. He approached the wagon's side leading Dusty by the reins. Tyson spoke first. "I've been figuring on this," he said. "Best thing could of happened was being tossed by that buckskin of yours." He slid his good hand out from the blanket. It surprised him that the big horse let him pet the tip of his nose. "Might never had that talk with you or heard that Scripture." He smiled. "Banged up as I am, I got time to think about my situation and what all needs to change."

Cowboy took Tyson's hand to shake. To him he said, "You can tell folks you're committed to follow the Word. You can say what you figure they expect to hear. You might even act in keeping with all that talk. For awhile anyway." He placed a big finger to his own chest. "Until the changes reach here, it means nothing. Remember, the Lord will always know your heart."

The slap of reins on horsehide jolted the caisson into motion. Cowboy watched the loaded wagon lumber down the roadway at a slow walk. Tyson's pinto had no trouble keeping apace. The wrangler mounted Dusty, turning him back toward the cut-off road to Mecklenburg. The buckskin's amble soon became a trot.

They loped the trail at an easy pace.

Their journey had begun.

Any Horse in Texas
Study Questions

1. Kid Tyson thought he was not good enough for God. What stories from the Bible can you think of where God loved people who did not deserve that love? Does anyone ever earn the love of God?

2. Can you think of people you've met who had a rough exterior to cover up hurts and pain from the past? How do you go about dealing with them?

3. Why was Cowboy kind to Kid Tyson after what Tyson had done to him? Would you have done the same? Why or why not?

Adam's Missing Rib

Boys hailing from Deep South states rode up the trail with more than just a love of grits, magnolia trees, and political passion. Their manner of speaking seemed both delightful to the ear and at times downright incomprehensible. The ordinary Texan riding beside them couldn't tell a scuppernong from pinto beans, or find a hushpuppy in a prairie dog town. Doubtful either he might locate Plum Nelly on a map.

But the Lone Star cowpunchers quickly understood what it was the Southerners meant by a blackberry winter. More than once a late season Georgia frost had shriveled all new growth of the not-yet-spring. Whole hillsides of blackberry buds withered there, wildly delaying that mid-summer sweet fruit. Texas was no different.

Cowboy wondered as he rode this part of the trail if the moderate last several days would continue to warm, or whether the hill country would be treated to one more morning's light freeze. That thought vanished completely as he rode Dusty across the small rise topped with the first Mexican Blue oaks he'd seen in months. The prickly pear patch huddled at their base was what the old *vaqueros* called *Lengua de Tigre*, the Tiger's Tongue. A narrow notch through the hillside allowed the railroad to pass through in a lazy curve. Beyond that, the northern edge of the Balcones

Headland spread out below to reveal a small cluster of buildings that formed the growing village of Leesburg.

Well past its edge and in the midst of the open country, a substantial windmill turned a slow rotation. Each blade gleamed in the morning's sunlight; all eighteen of them. Cowboy guessed it took more than a hundred acres to hold the entirety of stout cow pens he saw standing there. Each enclosure brimmed with milling livestock. The continuous low murmur of congregated bovines, interrupted by random bellows, could not be mistaken even at this distance.

In the hour it took the wrangler to reach the stockyard, he marveled at the scope of operation John Calvin Quinn built in these last several months. Mulling that thought, Cowboy realized he did not know for sure just how long he'd actually been gone.

Cowboy reined Dusty in next to that first large pen in their path. It baffled him somewhat that the enclosure contained only short-horned cattle: Herefords mostly, with a scattering of Red Angus, and handful of Santa Gertrudis. Not a single broadhorn could be seen anywhere he looked. All of these beeves appeared to be yearlings.

To his left, Cowboy heard a wagon creak under heavy burden. Two short-necked Breton draft horses pulled the load with alternating strain and ease. The driver called out a single word to them, in a tone that sounded European. They stopped at once. "Willkommen, mein herr," the man said. He continued in English once he saw this tall rider was, in fact, an *Amerikanisher.* "If you have come to buy the beef, we sell only to the meat houses up the railroad line." He pointed to the loading ramp next to the freight car on the tracks. The curved *squeeze* chute began to fill with hefty cattle, just now approaching the inclined steps and narrow deck. Four men strung along the fencing prodded the herd with wooden poles to keep them moving.

As Cowboy turned back from watching this maneuvering, the driver said, "If you're looking for work, we don't need men on horseback. Mr. Quinn wants the job done on foot and by wagon." He smiled with the satisfaction of knowing his employer would not have to deal with another Texas saddle tramp on the drift.

Cowboy acknowledged this information with a most thoughtful nod. He scanned the pens with a slow turn of his head. A dozen or so men hurried about performing various chores, two others on wagons, the rest afoot. "Where is Cal?" he asked. It delighted him that the driver flinched at his use of the boss's Christian name.

"He supervises the loadings today." Slapping the reins, the man all but huffed in farewell. Clearly he had wasted enough time in idle conversation. The waiting pair of chestnut-hued geldings leaned muscled chests into the leathers. A blow of air puffed from each large nostril. The wagon ambled forward as before.

Cowboy could feel the unmistakable sensation as the big buckskin began to tremble beneath the saddle. "I can smell it, too, Dusty," Cowboy said. The long familiar odor permeated his nose and sinus. It began a tangy dryness at the back of his throat. "Can't mistake the stench of this much cattle bunched together." The wrangler shook his head. "And not no dust this time to fill your nostrils for some relief. Close my eyes and I swear we're riding drag again behind some northbound herd."

The big horse paced anxiously, one step sideways followed two quick steps back. This signaled that Dusty, too, missed the rigors of pushing cattle across wide open prairie. For a moment they each clung to a bit of reverie before Cowboy turned his mount back toward the loading ramp.

Making his way past the now empty sorting pens, Cowboy watched the youngest man of Cal's outfit close each blocking gate behind the moving throng of beeves. Bumping one another and bawling loudly, they crowded down a narrowing walk way between substantial fences toward the chute. In groups of twenty or so, the cattle stumbled through the main gate opened ahead of them. Once inside this rounded corral Cowboy guessed to be the forcing pen, four men walked behind them swinging slowly shut the gate that squeezed them single file onto the ramp and then into the waiting railroad car.

Cowboy had never seen cattle loaded for transport before. At the end of the drives, he and most of the other drovers had already headed home with money in their pockets by the time this got done. So, he watched the goings-on now with a keen mix of curiosity and fascination. He also wondered how cattle confined like this might act any different from those cattle out in the open.

They didn't. The wrangler spotted the trouble-maker two full minutes before that fat brockle-faced steer erupted into sheer panic.

Any drover worth a day's wages and a full meal knows that, with such wide-set eyes poised on the sides of its skull, a cow can instantly view almost everything except what's directly behind. So when they repeatedly turn their heads back one way, then the other, then behind them again—it means they're nigh to being spooked. While the basic instinct is to follow other cattle in the herd, their greater instinct is survival. That means escape. The merest opening will do. Where no exit avails itself, frenzied bedlam soon follows.

Cattle all have good memories. The stirred up brockle-face couldn't recall ever being in this part of the pens before, only adding to his overall agitation. He stood immobilized for a moment while considering his uncertain situation. That's when mistakes were made. The youngest man in the work crew proved himself to be a flat-heeled cattle man at best. He took it upon himself to move the frozen steer along with a simultaneous shout, "get on, there," and the stiff whacking of the rump with a cane.

The boy might as well have fired a loaded artillery piece. The brockle-face rocketed some twenty feet toward the Hereford squeezed against the fence. Short but wide, she bawled when the steer vaulted across her hips with all four of his hooves. In another instant, the brockle-face managed to leap clear of the enclosure, scraping a big belly on the wooden top rail and making a wobbly landing in soft dirt. Seeing nothing between himself and those distant hilltops, the steer bolted in that far off direction.

Cowboy ignored the shouting and cussing that came from inside the pens. Twelve men racing on foot carrying only canes and long hickory staves likely would be no help. By his own instinct, Dusty jerked into action before the steer's first hoof hit the ground. At a dead gallop, Cowboy untied his lariat from the saddle. He used the rhythm of the buckskin's hoof beats to shake out a sizeable loop.

The escaping steer thrashed loudly through knee-high grass and vegetation bordering the feedlot. He did not hear the approach of horse and rider. His first indication being the rope tightening around his neck when it began to cut off his breathing. It took only minutes for Cowboy to lead the reluctant stray back through the nearest opened gate into an empty pen.

Cowboy feared that any man among the crew might become the object of the steer's unvented animosity. With a light tug of both reins, he backed Dusty into taking slack from the rope. The wrangler dropped to the ground, stepped to the brockle-face in three strides, and with a hand on each horn wrestled the somewhat confused bovine to the ground with an easy move. Cowboy simply said, "Now," and Dusty slackened the rope enough for the wrangler to slip it off the steer's head.

The gate opened to find John Calvin Quinn standing there: university educated, builder of the largest feedlot in Texas, heir to a sizeable railroad fortune, and a handsome yet down-to-earth man. Outfitted now in manure-covered boots, a dirt stained shirt, and rumpled canvas pants, he labored happily as a man of the workaday cattle world. "I knew that had to be *you*," he said to Cowboy, "the big hat, the buckskin horse, the thick moustache." He laughed in true merriment as he shut the gate behind exiting horse and rider. They shook hands with a grip that at once held warmth and the recognition of time passed since the last such occasion. "I swear, if it's not you wrestling down one of my horses, then it's you roping one of my fleeing cattle. Thank you for that." He slapped the wrangler on the shoulder. His grin almost touched both ears.

With a shout and a wave of the arm, Cal gathered the men around him. "Boys," he said to the gathering, "I'd like you to meet the fella that saved my life that misbegotten day I rode a loco'd horse into a clamorous town." The men nodded in various degrees of approval. "But more than just that," Cal continued, "this is the man who introduced me to Emma, and convinced me to hire her as my clerk." That brought a general whoop of appreciation and loud applause all around."

Cowboy realized that these men adored her the same as he did. Being taller than most, the wrangler could easily scan the entirety of the pens and buildings. He did not spot the named young lady any place about.

Cal noticed Cowboy's efforts. He offered, "Why don't you and I take a walk over to the office. I believe there is someone there who would very much like to see you." They ambled together in a comfortable stride, and in even easier conversation. Dusty trailed a few steps behind.

Ten yards from the building's porch both men halted when a door flew open without warning. A slender, auburn-haired figure stepped out, one hand touching the door frame. The loud gasp was immediate. "It *is* you!" she shrieked. In the few seconds it took to run the distance to where the two men stood, Emma became a fevered blur of flapping pigtail, pumping elbows, and a flurry of boots and jeans.

The excited impact of her head and shoulders slamming his chest almost bowled Cowboy over. Even though braced, he still needed a quick step behind him to maintain balance.

"You came back," she cried, "you really came back." Emma repeated those words over and again between sobs. Her muted tones emanated from somewhere buried around his midsection. For a long minute they stood this way: Emma crying hot tears of complete joy, Cowboy's arms cradling her warmly, and Cal watching them both with a growing fondness.

At last, Emma stood back a step to take an admiring look at her long-absent friend. She held both of his big hands in her much smaller ones.

Cal quit his big grin long enough to speak first. "If I were more of a jealous man, sir," he told Cowboy with obvious good cheer, "I would demand that you take your hands off my wife."

***

The mouse faces south. He stays a creature of clutter, but labors unceasingly to pursue order. The eagle flies east. From lofty heights he sees all. He was granted the gift of vision. The buffalo paws dirt in the north. His ample size suggests true abundance of those manifesting resolute action. The bear lumbers west. He seeks hibernation. His reclusive sleep reinvigorates him through peace and solitude. So the campfire storytellers told the other drovers about the circle of life.

Cowboy wondered why he recalled that yarn just now. For the better part of the last hour, he busied himself shoveling dried manure off the wagon onto freshly plowed ground. When he saw Emma smile at him from across the field he knew. The wrangler first met Emma in her uncle's big barn. At the time, he was shoveling manure into a wagon off of the dirt floor. His life, in this instance, had come full circle.

She walked up to the wagon. A wide apron was tied to her waist. She held the bottom corner of the cloth in each hand. In the deep pouch formed there, a full pile of potatoes cut to chunks jostled with each step. "Well," she said, "it's really not that much, but it was all I could find." With that announcement made, Emma dropped the load beside the wagon wheel.

"In the three days I been here, "Cowboy said, "you and Cal provided good company and fed me like a prince. Doing chores for the likes of you two is downright pleasurable. But I can't say as I become much of a farmer." He swept his hand to indicate her patch of turned earth in the midst of the nearby rolling tallgrass. "I expect as how you ain't got enough spud bits there to plant this entire acre."

"There you go funning me again," Emma laughed with lilting tones. "You remember Mrs. Hagebak? I roomed in her boarding house when I first got here." She looked at Cowboy as though he were a favorite yard dog come to get his ears scratched. "We became good friends. She got her nephew to plow a little plot for me as a favor." She laughed at the recollection. "I promised him a little money for his help, and shared with him that someday I'd have a huge garden. I came out here the next day to find he'd done all of this."

Cowboy nodded. In his mind he could watch that all play out. He tossed out the last of the wagon's load, jumping down beside the girl. "Where's Cal?" he asked. "Don't he get to help out, too?"

"No," she said. "He offered to. More than once, in fact. He did again this morning." Her face took on a look Cowboy had never seen before. Determination dissolved into an easy serenity. "Ever since I saw the garden that widow left my aunt and uncle when she sold them her husband's house near Cowtown, I wanted to learn how to work it." She looked in his eyes for a moment, knowing his connection to that old place. "Aunt Mildred kept me too busy doing my chores and all her work as well" I never did more than watch the weeds grow in that little spot by the barn." Her eyes lit up once more. "This will be my first real garden, so I wanted to start out small. And I wanted to do it by myself."

Cowboy removed a slender hickory stave from beneath the wagon's seat. He found a pile of them back at the feed lot. Using the knife from the back of his belt, the wrangler whittled a point to one end. If not exactly sharp, at least it became less dull. "How's it figure then," he asked, "that you got me out here with you?"

"Oh, I've always heard tell that cowboys are special," Emma teased. "I don't know about all that, but I know that you are." She placed her hand lightly on his elbow. "I wanted to spend some time today without having to share you. You'll be headed south soon enough."

The wrangler looked at the tip of the stave, seeing some final adjustment had to be made. He said, "And you reckon it wouldn't hurt none either if you was to work me some while you was at it."

"Well, there is that." She laughed at his suspicion. "What exactly are you're doing with that knife and stick?"

Cowboy shook the hickory in his hand. "Around here, y'all call this a cattle prod," Cowboy answered. "I intend to use it to keep from burying all those potato seeds in the dirt on my hands and knees." He picked up a potato piece to demonstrate. Grabbing the stave high on the shaft with point down, Cowboy hefted his hand to shoulder height. He rammed the point into the dirt, creating a hole deep enough for proper planting. Next he dropped in the potato, kicking soil back into the hole with the toe of his boot. "Just like Ma taught me when I was a kid," he said.

For the next two hours those steps were repeated: Emma would drop a potato eye where she wanted it planted. Cowboy would poke a hole next to it, nudge the potato in, and tamp dirt on top of it. They would stop only when Emma needed to get more bits from the pile near the wagon. They continued until all potatoes were buried.

Watching her walk back with that final load, Cowboy studied changes to the young woman he left behind those many months ago. Her hair still hung in a single braid tied with ribbon. It swept across one shoulder and tucked into the apron top. Now, Emma's face held a particular glow; almost a radiance. Her eyes nearly sparkled whenever she looked at him. More curious to Cowboy, a greater fullness had come to her cheeks and a bit more to her hips. Tanned skin gave off a certain healthy look.

"Mi *bonita*," he said, "I would say you been mostly happy since you come to Leesville."

"*Bonita?*" she asked half-mocking. "I thought your name for me was *mi chica.*" Her bright eyes began to focus somewhere in the distance. "But you are right, life got so much better since leaving Cowtown and moving here. I actually work harder, but it seems like nothing at all." Emma turned to face him once more. "And I met Cal," she said, letting the notion stand by itself. "I will always be thankful that you made that happen."

Before Cowboy could plead any denial, Emma shushed him with a wave of her hand. She picked up the small basket from her side of the wagon seat. It held a thick bundle inside a red-and-white checkered cloth. This she handed to Cowboy for him to hold while she spread a blanket at the edge of the plowed ground.

Emma sat on the cloth while Cowboy squatted on boot heels next to her. He took the pastry from her proffered hand, but did not recognize it at first glance. "Never seen one of these," he said. "If'n it's you who made it, I'll bet it's good." The wrangler took a long whiff of the concoction. He could smell the traces of cinnamon cooked in butter. It's rumpled crust felt soft in his fingers. At the first bite, Cowboy could taste the fruit.

"Boy howdy," he said through a mouth mostly full, "that is somethin'." A hard swallow followed. "How's it called?"

Emma beamed at the surprised but satisfied look on his face. "Mrs. Hagebak taught me," the young woman said. "She called it a skillet cake." Taking a tentative nibble, Emma said, "This one is made with pieces of dried apple." She offered up a second piece which he took without hesitation.

"You feed Cal like this?" Cowboy asked. "Not regular I reckon. He don't look none too fat." The wrangler wiped crumbs from the big mustache with the back of his knuckles. "How long is it since you got hitched?"

"Oh, it's been four months now," she replied.

"Well, shoot-fire!" he said. "I been gone that long?"

"Yes," Emma said evenly. "It's been a tad more than seven months since you rode north. Cal and I worked together every day after that getting it all organized, men hired, and materials delivered to site." Her air took on a matter-of-factness. "One noonday while I was eating dinner in the back of an empty buckboard, he found me reading from the Bible you gave me." She smiled remembering. "That started long conversations about Scripture. We grew closer every day after that. Two months later he proposed to me in the parlor of the boarding house."

"And then," Cowboy said, "y'all found a preacher and said vows."

"No," she said. "The next week his father came to Leesburg to inspect the feedlot operation. Being a railroad man rich as Croesus, I expected him to look down on our engagement." She smiled with a new found pride. "Not only was he accepting, he was welcoming. A man of God himself. He insisted we come to Chicago so I could meet the rest of Cal's family." She then gushed, "We even took our honeymoon in this big hotel by the Great Lake. It was like a fairytale."

Cowboy placed a hand on her shoulder. He squeezed gently. "I'm proud for you, Emma. Plain proud." He held the touch for long seconds. "Sounds like you got yourself a good man, and that your matrimony has turned life to the good." He chuckled to himself. Or thought he did, but she caught him.

"What's humorous about that?" she asked.

"You just didn't look like a gal dragging her rope when I left here, is all. Didn't figure marriage for you so soon."

"So soon?" She blurted those words at him. "I turned nineteen while you were gone. High time for a woman to settle in." Her eyes focused keenly on his. "I was lead to this man by Providence. Something that I could not, nor would not ignore." She drew a defiant breath. "And what about you?"

"Me?" He answered in true perplexity.

She said, "You're not a spring foal any more, and it would break my heart if I thought you were just to drift about the rest of your days." Moisture began to well at the corner of each eye.

"Don't worry, *mi chica*," Cowboy reassured her. "A year ago, likely I woulda busted out at your remark." He stood up to full height, and extended a hand to her. With almost no effort the wrangler raised Emma off the blanket. "Thing is, I barely have eight years on you. Still young enough for a good woman to find worth courting." His face eased into a sober reflection. "Spending that day hiding in the cave with a bear trying to eat me has made me think on what I should do in this life. Settling down is a particular notion I intend to take up one day."

He folded the blanket, and placed it next to the basket on the wagon seat. "Wedlock," he said, "seems to do well by you and Cal. It gives me encouragement."

"Remember," Emma said, "In the Book of Genesis it was God who said 'It is not good for the man to be alone.' That was the first thing in Creation He said was not good. So God made woman to be Adam's companion and helper."

At her straightforward use of Scripture, Cowboy flashed a prideful smile. He pleasantly acknowledged, "As I recall Adam had to give up a rib in that bargain." His impish facade gave away his intent.

"Now you're just joshing me," she said. "It's not that Adam's rib just went missing. More like a marriage partner was found for him." Her smile matched his good humor.

"You'd give up a little flesh and bone for a good wife, would you not?"

"Reckon that story gets told when I meet her," Cowboy said. "Afore that happens, I got to get right with the family back home. Done 'em a bad turn years back. *Corazón contrito*, a contrite heart and some *grande* restitution is what's called for."

He threw the remaining gardening gear in the back of the wagon. In a moment more, he helped Emma into her seat, took his, and slapped the horses into a fast walk. The wrangler turned when he felt her staring at him. She said, "You came back like you said you would. You kept your promise." It made her feel good just to say those words. "When you come back this way again it will be without such obligation." Emma leaned into him a bit without waiting for the road to jostle them together. "Know that you will always be welcome." She whispered barely above the creaking wagon sounds, but Cowboy already felt the warmth of her words down in his soul.

They rode home in happy silence.

***

"The only way to the mountaintop begins with a first step up that hill." With those words, Cowboy's Pa would extol his boys to a greater effort whenever their stamina began to flag. The wrangler knew that his Pa would never judge this modest knoll rising from the otherwise flat land to be a true mountain. Just the same, standing in front of the newly constructed clapboard house, it afforded Cowboy a pleasant view of the feedlot slightly less than two miles distant. The garden stretched out behind them over a slight decline.

Cal stood next to Cowboy as the wrangler tied bedroll and saddle bags on Dusty. Emma continuously came back and forth from the building's open doorway. With each trip she brought more essentials for the tall rider to carry with him down the trail. Foodstuffs mostly, but also a newly cut wind-rag with her fancy stitching on all sides, and a passel of handwritten notes Emma had composed to Cowboy in his absence. She had no clue where to send them in his absence; an old hatbox held them until his return. Emma asked him to only read those posts whenever he stopped to build a campfire at day's end.

"Whatever else could she possibly load Dusty down with?" Cowboy asked his friend. "She brings much more, I will have to fill the saddle's seat and walk my buckskin back to Atascosa." Both men laughed. The horse turned his head to them. His look all but said that the buckskin found little humor in their talk, except that he, too, had grown fond of Emma. Dusty already smelled the bag of corn dodgers she brought on the last trip; his particular favorite.

"I must tell you," Cal began, "that I really love this woman." He looked up into the wrangler's watchful eyes. "Emma has been a true blessing in my life. Not only is she a steadfast and gentle companion, but this pretty little lady keeps me moving on the right road." He looked back at the door in anticipation. "And, I must confess, Emma has stopped me from doing some plain foolish things."

Cowboy raised a single eyebrow in reply.

Color touched cheek tops as Cal continued, "I was just about to buy the *only* pair of albino breeding mules in all of Texas when Emma came back into the office. Instead of just throwing the charlatan out, she surprised me by asking what else he had." Cal's hand pointed to the fenced opening of the barn. "For a dollar he sold us that: Cinnamon, her one-eyed pony." The tiny gray mare rubbed a shoulder back and forth against the wood.

"I swear," Cal said. "Some days Emma dotes on that animal almost more than she does me." He smiled with true affection. "Another reason just to take her in your arms and hug her."

His face turned serious now. "As I spoke on it last evening," Cal said, "I could use you here to help me run things." He hesitated awkwardly. "If south Texas holds nothing more for you, please come back." He gauged the wrangler's brief consideration of this proposal, sensing only a bit of relief at the offer but no commitment.

"Thank you, kindly," Cowboy returned. "I intend to make Atascosa my future. Whatever that might be."

"Then consider this," Cal continued. "You know cattle: good ones, tolerable ones, and in my business the ones to stay away from. Right now I have no buyer's agent in that part of the state. But the demand for beef back East has yet to slacken."

Cowboy laughed. "I would be stealing your money, Cal, if I was to ride around most days saying, 'Buy that one and that one, let that one that one go'." He let his gaze wander in the direction of the distant feed lot. "Any puncher with an ounce of savvy could do that, and at half the pay."

Emma stepped out on the porch with the last of her bundles. "Just give it some thought," Cal said, slapping the big man on the shoulder. "You can telegraph me here if you change your mind."

Cowboy took the bundle in one large hand, He could feel the warmth of fresh baked goods even through the thick cloth. "What is this, then?" he asked. "More sweet victuals I don't have to share with Cal?"

"They're called *Āebleskiver,*" Emma said with a laugh. "It's how the Danish make their doughnuts in the old country. Sailors took them on long voyages, so these might last until you get home." Her eyes reminded the wrangler of his Ma's last look at him when he mounted up for that first cattle drive years ago. Her tears quickly followed. She grabbed Cal's arm to steady her, but could find no words.

Sensing this, Cal took charge. "Emma wants, we both want, you to come back this way for at a visit from time to time." The man removed the hat from his head. "Maybe at the end summer — or the fall at the latest," Cal waited for Emma to find her voice before continuing, "Say for certain you'll come back to see the three of us then."

Cowboy bobbed his head in agreement as the younger man spoke his piece. He stopped mid-nod to digest those last few words. "What three of you?" he asked in all sincere puzzlement.

Cal grinned then with unbridled enthusiasm. "Well, sir, Emma is with child. The baby will come by summertime." Emma blushed at that announcement, but smiled weakly just the same. Cal put his arm around her for as much assurance as affection.

"That is right fine news," the wrangler said. He removed his big hat this time. "I'd be proud to come see what the Lord has blessed you with. Nothing in this world could keep me from it."

He shook Cal's hand in congratulations, and waited for the bear hug he knew was coming. Emma embraced him much stronger than when he left months ago to ride north.

"One last thing before you go," Emma spoke in a voice just recovering its strength. "I bit my tongue up 'til now, but I cannot let you ride off until I know."

"What might that be?" Cowboy asked.

"Cal and I only refer to you as '*the* cowboy' or '*that* cowboy'," she said. "We don't even know your name. We're not supposed to ask that of a man out here, but please won't you tell me."

Cowboy smiled. Without hesitation, he told both of them.

"That's beautiful," Emma said. Upon reflection, she continued, "If it's a boy, we'll give him your first name. If it's a girl, we'll give her your middle name. That is, if you don't mind."

Cowboy stood mute just trying to find his breath again. Before he could utter anything, Cal chimed in. "An excellent idea," he exclaimed. "Say you agree."

At last Cowboy said, "I don't have the words, so a simple 'yes' will have to make do." More hugs and handshakes followed. Dusty watched the unfolding folderol with patient dark eyes.

At last, Cowboy stepped into the saddle. He swept the hat still in his hand along the horizon from the busy railroad, to full cow pens, to freshly plowed ground. "God bless your family, and all He helped you build."

Cowboy turned the buckskin south, looking back one last time before the ground sloped behind a tree-topped rise. He eased Dusty into a trot.

They loped the trail at an easy pace.

Their journey had begun.

Adam's Missing Rib
Study Questions

1. When the steer ran from the loading process, Cowboy and Dusty sprang to action, roping him and bringing him back to his rightful place. Cowboy also used his know-how to help make potato planting easier. What skills has God given you that you can use for the good of other people? What skills can you work on to make them better and more useful to serve others?

2. Emma and Cal's relationship began when Cal found Emma reading the Bible from Cowboy. How can relationships be based on Scripture? Are your closest relationships with other Christians who make your walk with Jesus closer? Why or why not?

3. Cowboy's journey, and particularly his time with the bear, made him think about his direction in life. Emma quotes Genesis to Cowboy about it not being good for a man to be alone. Is pursuing marriage the right decision for everyone? Why or why not? If you are married, are you giving up yourself each day for your spouse? What are some ways you can better serve your spouse?

4. Emma and Cal had love for each other that was not based on how each person behaved. How is the love that Emma and Cal have like the love Jesus has for us? Do you love people more based on what they do than on who they are? How can you show love that is more like Jesus' love?

Remember No More

Legends about wind captured Cowboy's interest like no other: the names for it, the power of it, and even causes for the absence of it. Didn't matter, he would listen to any and all accounts with rapt attention. From the vaqueros on the trail he learned that a man standing with his back to the wind could know with certainty that storms would only come from his left-hand side. Near the mountains along the Great Plains, people told him winter's eastbound winds were dubbed the *Snow Eaters*. Stories there told of mid-winter currents rushing down the slopes so balmy that four feet of snow melted in a single afternoon. One old-timer claimed he'd been driving a buckboard into town, his team barely keeping pace with that blustery warm wind. His pair of horses was running chest-deep in snow, but the wheels were already axle-deep in mud. And, the cow pulled behind the wagon kicked up only dust.

Fanciful yarn as that account seemed, Cowboy instead could only concentrate on a story he'd been told that one night by Isaac Coverdale. It bothered the wrangler greatly that he could not fathom why this recitation rolled over and again in the back of his mind, almost without ceasing. Before his death, Cousin Charlie shared a tale told around the Isle of Cuba. It spoke of how the doldrums, that almost complete lack of wind, caused sailors traveling there to name that part of the ocean the Horse Latitudes. By tradition, English sailors were given a month's wages days before setting out to sea. Most frittered that away on liquor and lewd behavior; this wastefulness termed "the dead horse" for reasons not fully explained by young Charlie. After thirty day's sail, most ships reached the Caribbean with its relative windless waters. With little to do in this calm and also to celebrate their freedom from debt, sailors would weave together horse-figures made of straw. They delighted in beating them with a stick before throwing the remains overboard, bidding farewell to their financial burden. That sight Cowboy likely would never see, but he hoped one day to fully understand the meaning of this tale.

The wrangler stood from squatting on boot heels next to the base of the town's Axtell windmill. Watching eighteen slanted blades turned by a slow breeze to draw ground water had unexpectedly begun the wrangler's dreamy recollections. Now, Dusty finished drinking from the mill's water trough. Rather than saddle up to ride those last sixty miles toward Atascosa, Cowboy ambled toward Schulenburg's main street, leading the big horse by the reins. He calculated they faced two more campfires together before reaching the outskirts of home. His coffee tin barely held half a spoonful of stale ground beans.

Of greater concern to the wrangler, this small town held the last public bath and barber shop this side of the family's old ranch. Cowboy judged that if he needed to eat a large heap of crow in coming days, best to shake Texas from his boots and scalp before he did so. To reach the first of the two dozen or so mercantile buildings—all wood-constructed, one-story, and standing free of each other—Cowboy had to cross a somewhat wide expanse of well-trampled dirt. No signage indicated whether that tract belonged to any one man, but that probably didn't matter. Cowboy smiled as he remembered how very little land cost south of San Antone.

He counted four wagons, each pulled by pairs of stout horses. The closest stood in front of a building marked "Outfitters". Another rested next to the squarish white-washed store with the block-lettered sign proclaiming: "W. M. Vinson Groceries". The third stood all but abandoned in the middle of the thoroughfare. And the last wagon had halted in front of a building whose sign lay in unreadable shadow.

A group of men gathered at one establishment's arched entry. Built entirely of limestone blocks, it sat squat and substantial on the corner. The rough, light-colored exterior seemed out of place this far from the Hill Country. It surprised Cowboy not the slightest that this housed the Merchant & Farmers Bank.

Horse and rider sauntered across the wide street, headed directly for the grocery at the far end. Cowboy expected to purchase more Arbuckle coffee, maybe a confection or two as a gift for the family, and be on his way in short order. Taking his time to enjoy the faint sunshine that poked through overcast skies, Cowboy felt the mild breeze brush his cheeks. Spring was coming.

Cowboy chanced to read that sign hidden before by shadow. The building belonged to a law office, the esquire's name painted in crisp black letters: "Riley Culpepper — Attorney at Law". The wrangler read the words aloud, in a voice now as unsteady as his disquieted spirit had become. The wrangler's entire body flashed an immediate sweat. Cowboy stood frozen in the middle of the street. He would have remained so for more long moments had Dusty not snorted at him with either impatience or questioning.

His mount tugged at the reins, jostling Cowboy out of his near trance.

"By Josh and Joan, Dusty," he said to his horse, "I haven't spoke that name since I cussed the boy and busted his jaw." Cowboy looked at the buckskin and back to the sign. "If it be him," the wrangler continued. "But how many men in these parts could have that name?" Cowboy shook his head a long moment. "A lawyer makes money with his mouth—and a ten-gallon one at that. Trifle hard to do when it's all stove up bad like his was, last time I seen it."

The big man squinted at the space in the glass between the partially raised shade and the somewhat fancy cafe curtain covering the window's bottom half. Sunshine's glare across the pane prevented Cowboy from viewing the room behind. He swallowed hard once, and let out a long breath. At last the wrangler took the few steps to the post where he tied up Dusty.

After another moment, Cowboy crossed the wooden walkway only to find the door locked when he tried to turn the shiny embellished knob. Before he could let go of that brass, a man who'd been standing with the others in front of the limestones called out to him. "If you're looking for the lawyer," he said, "Culpepper's down at the bank. He always spends Wednesday at Merchants and Farmers."

To the man about to resume his walk down the street, Cowboy called back out, "How best to recognize him, mister? Don't know that I've ever laid eyes this fella."

"Easy enough," he replied. "Wears a striped gray vest, white shirt, and cattleman's black string tie."

Cowboy nodded his thanks. He slapped the buckskin's rump on his way past, headed to the bank. In the two minutes it took to cross the broken dirt street, the wrangler could find no words suitable to say if, in fact, *this* Riley Culpepper was his one-time nemesis.

The bank lobby proved as much a bulwark as the exterior seemed to be. A polished wooden facade took up one wall. Behind two black metal screens, clerks in suspenders and bowties helped townspeople with their money matters. Near a small barred window, a single desk and two wooden chairs nestled in the tiny remaining space. Sitting there, a man dressed as the stranger in the street suggested sat leafing through a stack of papers.

Cowboy studied the man, finding nothing familiar. The hair was too dark, the body too slender. When the man stood to reach a portfolio atop a nearby cabinet, he seemed too tall to be that chubby kid the wrangler remembered.

Turning back to his desk, the man noticed Cowboy standing there for the first time. The wrangler stared hard at him, not bothering to hide it at all. "May I help you, sir?" the man asked with practiced pleasantry. "Is this your first visit to our bank? Your first time in Schulenburg?"

When Cowboy heard him speak, in an instant he could recall listening to that voice in a hundred conversations, most of them harsh. To Riley he said, "You Strack Culpepper's boy, the one we all called *Pudge*?"

For a long and soundless second the man only blinked eyes in wonderment and curiosity. "Well saints alive," Culpepper laughed, "I haven't been called that in years. Used to be quite the fatso as a young'un." He now focused on Cowboy, but could not place this stranger from days since passed. "I don't recognize the mustache, or the hat. Maybe the eyes a little," he let that trail off, still trying to call this man to mind. Not until the wrangler stepped closer toward the desk did any memory flicker in Culpepper's head. "That walk," he said in a rush of breath. A budding recollection began to unsettle him.

"The last time I saw a man walk like that, it ended in a severe whupping for me." It was Culpepper's turn to swallow hard. "Lord save us," he whispered. "You're little Johnny's big brother." The man went more pale than his starched white shirt. "You come here like you promised one day you would? You come back to finish that beating?" Silence filled the space between them.

***

When faced with fearsome threats to the tribe, the peace-loving native peoples of south central Texas knew that they could just take off running and hope for the best. Or else the tribe could stand and fight with those few weapons they had at hand. Instead, venerable elders of the Coahuiltecans [kwa WEEL teh kens] band, living on the banks of the San Antonio River, counseled a third option: strike a truce with the attackers and abide with the terms. Better to live in a forced friendship than lose blood on a knife's edge or die at the sharp end of a warrior's lance. But the Europeans marching north in search of gold posed a much different menace. The Conquistadors cared nothing for tribute payments of crops or livestock. Rather they wanted accommodating citizens for their new colonies. But neither the soldiers nor the Franciscan monks among their number spoke any of the seven Coahuiltecan dialects. Tribal leaders viewed these Spaniards with equal parts apprehension, wariness, and suspicion.

Cowboy calculated that was the same look he now saw on Riley Culpepper's face. The young attorney sat behind a polished oak desk in his law office, shelf upon shelf of imposing leather bound books stood stacked behind him. He listened as the wrangler finished telling a story of life on the trail.

"You'll have to give me a moment here," Culpepper said. He poured water from a hobnail glass pitcher into one of the four matching tumblers. This he handed to Cowboy before filling the second for himself. After two swallows, he set the glass down and said, "Did I hear you say that you rode out of Atascosa County never to return because you were afraid of *me*?" Culpepper pushed himself back more against the padded chair as though to further distance himself from a rattlesnake he just discovered coiled in a corner.

"I was between hay and grass back then, a boy growing to a man," Cowboy said. "More fists than brains. The pure Simon truth of it, I figured busting a man's jaw like I did is like breaking a pony's leg. It ruins him for life." He shook his head with eyes screwed shut, remembering the shame he created. "A man can't eat, can't really talk; and the disfigurement lasts forever." The wrangler opened his eyes to face Culpepper once more. He struggled to square that harsh memory with what now sat before him.

A smile of untold relief spread across Culpepper's face. "As you can see," he said while running the fingers of his right hand along the jaw. "Even in this shadowed light, my face is just fine. Handsome even." Culpepper laughed at Cowboy's apparent discomfort as much as at his own half-playful attempt to buck himself up.

"But I broke it," Cowboy said. "I seen that when you was lying in the dirt trying to regain your senses."

Culpepper nodded. "I thought it was, too," he said. "I couldn't open my mouth, nor close it either. Hurt clear down to my shoulders." He put a palm flat against the jaw to test it one more time. "My folks took me to old Doc Crenshaw. After fussing around a bit, he told me to look at the ceiling. Then he stuck a big thumb under my tongue and grabbed my chin with those stubby fingers of his." Culpepper squinted as he thought of that night again. "He yanked hard. All I could see was stars in my eyes through falling tears. Before I could even take breath to scream, he yanked again. Harder. This time it sounded like someone snapped a dried pulley bone, but the jaw popped back into place. Out of joint, it seems. Not broke." He demonstrated this to Cowboy by flexing and closing his lower jaw. "Works just fine," he announced with guarded satisfaction.

"Your ma and pa must have been angry as hornets," Cowboy said, "When they seen it was me done this to you. My family owed money to your pa's bank for the ranch, and he never seemed a forgiving man."

A long silence hung between them for the second time that day as Riley Culpepper gathered the words he needed to say. "I never told my parents about the fight," he said finally, in a quiet almost matter-of-fact tone. "Pa thought I just fell off my horse again," he went on, "landing on my chin this time."

"What?!" Cowboy choked out in a whisper.

He stood up so fast that his now empty chair fell back on the plank floor behind him. In a moment more, his eyes grew to the size of Morgan dollars, but the look turned inward. It did not see the young lawyer with both hands now flat on the fancy oak.

"You mean," Cowboy said, halting between each incredulous word. "I didn't need to..." The import of Culpepper's words hit the wrangler like a mule's kick to the gut. It took breath away. He sat down hard on the chair he pained to upright.

When wits returned, Cowboy simply asked Culpepper, "Why not?" He could not fathom any reasonable explanation.

"If you recall," Culpepper said, "you kicked dirt on my chest with your boots as I lie there. When I refused to get back up, you told me, 'If you ain't learned the lesson yet, Pudge, I'll sure to come back and finish it." He smiled at Cowboy, estimating there would be no further fisticuffs. "So, it was me that was actually afraid of you." He chuckled at bit at the notion. "We both left that occasion with reason to avoid the other. Too bad it took all these years to put it behind us." His look turned a bit sober now. "We've put an end to it now, haven't we?"

"No," Cowboy said.

Firmness in his voice left no doubt it was not over for him. The big man stood to lean part way across the lawyer's desk. This startled Culpepper until he saw Cowboy stick out a big hand to shake. He noticed, too, the tears that welled up and rolled slowly from the wrangler's eyes.

"I owe you a sincere apology," Cowboy said, "for bustin' you up like that, and causing such pain as you had to endure. I beg you to forgive me that. And I beg you to forgive me leaving without saying a word or owning up to what I done." He shook his head at the thought of his own shortcomings. "I took the coward's way out that day. Got on a horse and rode away."

Riley Culpepper seized the outstretched hand firmly as he, too, stood. "No one could ever say it wasn't a fair fight," he said. "I started it with all that childish taunting. I even swung first." He grinned. "The whole thing might have turned out differently if I had actually hit you." Both men laughed heartily at that. "In my mind," Culpepper continued, "there is no need, but without hesitation I will tell you that you are forgiven."

***

Most Nez Perce warriors had spotted fever.

Not that sickness of the body, but the liking for a breed of horse with spotted skin and white rumps: the Appaloosa. These lean horses of the Wallowa Valley herd excelled at enduring long rides over rough terrain. The tribe prized them for the ability to jump barriers with relative ease. Yet every Nez Perce also knew of the horse's iron spirit. Any Appaloosa would grudgingly let a human ride its back, but only as long as it suited him.

Cowboy and Culpepper stood in front of the first gated stall. The big barn doors swung out onto the town's main street. An opening at the back gave way to a small corral behind the building. The motionless Appaloosa stud stared back at both men through shiny black eyes. The muscles beneath its tough hide all but quivered as the horse restrained its tremendous energy.

"I know for a fact," said Cowboy, "the U.S. Cavalry thought them Nez Perce up in Idaho was fierce fighters." He laughed as he turned to the lawyer. "A lieutenant once told me that's 'cuz by the time they got to the battle after struggling to ride those headstrong Appaloosa, the warriors was already mad as wet hens. They just took it out on the enemy."

"Is that really true?" Culpepper asked, doubtful tones creeping in his question. "Or, you just funnin' me?"

"Well," Cowboy said, "most wranglers wouldn't pick 'em out of a *remuda* for that day's ride, if another hoss was available."

The wrangler stuck out a hand toward the horse's lip. He wanted to see the teeth, but the Appaloosa pulled its head aside. It took neither a step sideways nor a step back.

Instead, the Appaloosa stood its ground. The look all but dared Cowboy to try that again.

"Seems a mite contrary," Cowboy said after a moment's consideration. "Got a rodeo on your hands with that one. Gonna take a top hand to ride him, for sure." He eyed the stallion a few seconds more, then said, "I'd let him be." Riley Culpepper nodded his agreement.

Both men moved on to the next stall. A scruffy sorrel mare stood at the back end of the enclosure. Her ears lay back flat, head lowered slightly, moving slowly side to side. Sweat gleaned off the ewed-neck, taking on its somewhat reddish hue. "No good horse comes in a bad color," Cowboy said without breaking stride, "but that dampness makes her look as dark as her mood. I'd wager she's only green broke, and got ridden hard to take the fight out afore you come." Cowboy continued walking with an easy stride. Over his shoulder he called to Culpepper, "How much does this hombre owe you?" he asked, "'cause what we seen so far ain't no top horse." The lawyer smiled but said nothing in return.

Cowboy stopped so abruptly at the third stall that Culpepper, still eyeballing the mare, almost ran into him. "Well I'll be cussed," the wrangler said, taking the full measure of what he saw. "Not seen nuther of these since Hector was a pup." The wrangler pointed with a slight ballyhoo to the brawny horse in the small confines. When Cowboy saw that this meant nothing to the lawyer, he said, "I'm figuring this to be that Mustang-Morgan mix." Even that drew no recognition from Culpepper, so he continued in growing annoyance, "Like the horse named *Comanche*, the only living thing to survive the Little Big Horn." Cowboy gazed at the horse now with some intensity. "You don't see them much down this way, if it ain't pulling cavalry wagon." He nodded at the fenced rear doorway. "Let's take a look-see at him in the open."

While Culpepper unlatched the entry into the corral, Cowboy eased the stall's gate open. He stood to one side, awaiting which direction the Morgan would take, and how fast he'd go to get there. To the wrangler's satisfaction, the horse ambled at a leisurely walk to the open dirt of the paddock. Once there, he circled the enclosure twice with purposeful methodic steps. Had the two men not stepped into his path the horse might have continued that walk the remainder of the day.

"Take this leather," Cowboy said, directing Culpepper toward the stout animal. "Let's see how easy he takes to being haltered." The wrangler smiled. "Remember: ask a mare, tell a gelding, and bargain with a stallion. You're halfway there, he's already had the knife."

The Morgan stood some inches less in height than Dusty, but made up that shortfall in girth. His barrel of a chest stretched a quarter again as wide as the buckskin. Built like a locomotive's steam engine, the horse was long and round. From breast to hindquarters, the mass of muscled flesh bespoke the powerhouse he must be.

The young lawyer approached with caution, but did so with a confidence that surprised Cowboy. Without fuss or struggle, he buckled the crown strap into place. In a moment more Culpepper adjusted the cheek piece to fit the Morgan's sturdy jaw line. Finally, the man turned back to the wrangler with a grin evidencing his satisfaction at both the choice of mount and his seeming rapport with the animal.

"Don't look like he's the kind to spit the bit." Cowboy said. "That's sure. Now let's see how he takes to having a rider." The wrangler stepped forward to give a helpful leg-up, but Culpepper waived him off.

"How can I claim to be Texan if I can't mount a horse by myself?" Culpepper said. With those words, he grabbed a handful of mane just above the withers, flexed knees, and launched himself into a leap. The lawyer landed in the thud of a tremendous belly flop across the Morgan's back. With a twist and a quick jerk, Culpepper threw a leg over the horse's wide hips. Then he pulled himself up to sit astride the animal.

Another grin danced its way across Culpepper's face when he realized the Morgan did not try to buck him off. He nudged both heels into flanks, and in return got the horse to resume its circuit of the corral. Cowboy walked along side for part of that way.

"Henceforth," the lawyer shouted with glee down to Cowboy, "I shall call him Hadrian. He certainly makes me feel like a Roman emperor sitting up here." The sight of it, and that proud announcement, made Cowboy recall his old saddle pal from England; the one they all called Professor. He, too, was given to unexpected theatrics. The wrangler watched horse and rider round the fence line twice more before Culpepper finally halted the newly named Hadrian and slid himself to the ground.

Brimming now with unfettered enthusiasm, the young lawyer strode next to Cowboy. Culpepper reached out with a thin hand to slap the wrangler across one shoulder. He said, "You and your family have been a source of unending inspiration for me. And today is just more proof of that." He indicated the Morgan now poised in a restful stance, eyeing both of them with an unhurried curiosity.

"I reckon I don't know the meaning of them words," Cowboy said. "How come you to say that?"

"It took a full six months or so for me to realize it," Culpepper said. "If I hadn't suffered the beating that day, likely I would have continued on as the person you so rightly described." He nodded to Cowboy in affirmation. "In fact, I was fat, and I was lazy. I pretended to be some local big shot, but I was only living in my father's shadow." He shoved his hands in pants pockets to level a steady gaze at Cowboy. "I've since believed that big right hand of yours crossing my chin just pointed it in the direction I should be going." Culpepper shrugged, and cocked his head slightly to one side. "After that, to the surprise of both my folks, I settled into a life of hard work. I learned the banking business up from clerk to board member. And seizing the opportunity when it happened, I read law with a retired judge in Austin."

Cowboy stared speechless. He tried more than once, but no words came. Culpepper swept his hands from hat to boots. "Everything you see here today," the young lawyer said, "began with me picking myself out of the dirt that day, after the fight ended."

The wrangler took this news like some drifter finding cake in place of grits on a breakfast plate. It perplexed him. He asked, "You spoke of my whole family. How's that?"

"You might not know of it," Culpepper said, "riding throughout the wilds as you did. Several years ago there was a substantial panic. Most of it back East, but we felt it here, too. Businesses failed, families ruined, banks in doubt." His brow furrowed at the sheer recollection of it. "Every man jack citizen in Atascosa wanted money in hand, so as to feel safe. Obviously banks didn't have cash on hand to do that." He flashed a pleasant look; put a light hand on Cowboy's elbow. "Your father was one of the voices that cautioned folks not to be so foolish. Ruining the bank would not get their money back, he told them." Culpepper spoke now with tones of true appreciation.

"Your father the preacher, and a few precious others, saved my family's bank."

Cowboy mustered an unconscious intensity without thinking. He stared off hard at nothing at all, not moving except for drawing breath. Seeing the big man in this state, Culpepper spoke out in calm tones, "Looks like you could use a hot meal and a good night's sleep. Let's put up ol' Hadrian here and head over to the café."

They did so.

Along the way, Culpepper said, "If you don't much dawdle on the trail betwixt here an Atascosa, you'll be at the home place by Saturday." He bent closer as his eyes foretold a secret bout to be shared. "That's your mother's birthday."

"How in blazes did you know that?" Cowboy shot back, coming out of his heretofore stunned silence.

"Oh, Marcus told me about a month ago," the young lawyer responded with all earnestness. "Your brothers and their wives will be there. You showing up for the occasion will just bless her heart."

"Wives?" Cowboy said as if stepping back into a sluggish dream. To his way of thinking, Marcus, Lucky, and Little Johnny were still mere boys. He doubted they'd grown an inch since he left.

"Why yes," Culpepper continued. "In fact, your youngest brother married Alice."

At this, Cowboy stopped short in the midst of the broken dirt street. He whirled on Culpepper, grabbing up a handful of the man's shirt along the forearm. "You mean," he said, "Johnny's hitched to your kid sister?"

"Yes," Culpepper said a second time. "That makes us almost like brothers-in-law." He chuckled in bemusement at the big man seeming so staggered to learn that life in Atascosa went on without his being there. After a few more paces towards the supper table, Culpepper said,

"Not only did you return to find yourself forgiven, you find yourself welcome, and back in the bosom of family. For better or worse, that now includes me."

Cowboy looked down at the shorter Culpepper once again, budding acceptance and dawning relief in his heart. To Cowboy Culpepper said, "I attended Marcus's church in Uvalde one Sunday. He seemed to look right at me when he quoted the verse. Psalm 32: 'Blessed is the one whose transgressions are forgiven, whose sins are covered. Blessed is the one whose sin the Lord does not count against them, and in whose spirit there is no deceit.' I came right home and put it to memory."

They stepped onto the wooden walkway running the length of the café. Cowboy grabbed the door's knob, but stopped his turn midway. The wrangler turned to face a bemused Culpepper. The meaning of the afternoon's conversation with the young lawyer, his once sworn enemy, began finally to sink in. Cowboy looked deep into Culpepper's eyes. "So," the big man said, "Ma and pa still own their ranch?"

Culpepper squinted in a most genuine perplexity. "That's right," he said. In a second more the lawyer added, "Mighty silly question. Why do you ask?"

***

In the minutes after dawning, Cowboy squat on boot heels next to a grove of mesquite at the edge of Schulenburg. A clump of bushes already beginning to bud lay huddled next to the trees' scaly trunks. The cowman watched a dozen yellow-eyed grackles plumed with pitch-black feathers scratch through the sparse vegetation. Ear-splitting cries filled the cool morning until a lead bird called the flock elsewhere. Cowboy mounted the buckskin when he saw Culpepper approach riding the docile beast now known as Hadrian.

"Mornin'," the lawyer said in most good cheer. "I came to wish you a fair and safe journey." He halted the stout gelding, almost touching Cowboy's mount. The men shook hands in silence for a long moment.

Cowboy spoke first. "I told Dusty just at first light," he said, "events of the day just past may have been a conjuring, or perhaps a dream. When I seen you ride up on that sizeable warhorse, I knew it to be for-a-fact actual." He took a broken red stone from the range coat's pocket. The wrangler had collected it off the canyon floor of the Talking Wall in Arapahoe country. This he held up for Culpepper to see.

"Near where this fell." he said, "I learned native warriors of the Plains tribes pray for great strength. Not to be superior to their brothers, but so that they can fight their fiercest enemy — themselves." Cowboy handed the rock to the young lawyer. "Take this as a keepsake to remember that." Cowboy's face eased from philosophical to sober. He said, "If yesterday was a rematch between us, I'm the one got whupped. Just the same, I take heart in the notion that I have to fight myself no longer." He grinned in quiet contentedness. "I was lead to you before reaching home. The work of Providence, no doubt. I am now a free man, and that feels good."

They shook once more. Before Cowboy could release the grip, Culpepper pulled him near, saying, "The gold you showed me last night: that's a second secret we shall both keep, just like the fight we never had. I'll get you better than a fair price and tell no one how you came by that money in your account. Deal?"

Cowboy nodded without word, recognizing the generosity of Culpepper's offer. The young lawyer finished with, "And I'll get that factory-made rig shipped home like you asked."

Cowboy turned the buckskin south towards the track leading to Atascosa. Dusty's walk became a trot.

They loped the trail at an easy pace.

Their journey *home* had begun.

Remember No More
Study Questions

1. Culpepper quickly forgave Cowboy when he asked forgiveness for the fight. Do you find it hard to forgive? How was Culpepper able to forgive so easily?

2. Culpepper's explanation of how the fight changed the direction of his life made Cowboy speechless. Tell a story about a time something bad happened to you that God used for good in your life.

3. Cowboy decided to fight himself no longer after talking with Culpepper. What fights have you had with yourself? How can you make your heart like the Morgan, under your control, instead of like the Appaloosa, that fights back constantly?

Nonesuch

All manner of south Texas predators, those who feed only in darkness, had long since fled to their dens. Even the many night birds gave up trilling and warbling as the blackened skies along the horizon's eastern flat began to purple, then to gray. Only the relentless mockingbird continued unending crying, still seeking to protect its territory or to seek a mate. When the dawn did come, it would be to Cowboy's back as he sat legs folded on matted earth next to a slender scrub oak. Behind him his buckskin foraged sprouts and other succulent new growth near the scaly tree's tangled roots.

In the slow-coming first light, a solitary barn cat, returning from the night's hunt, crossed open land stretched out before the wrangler. His crossing did not go unnoticed by either Cowboy or by that ever vigilant feathered mocker. With cries of warning, threat, and self-righteous anger, the slender bird swooped down to barrage the tom time and time again.

Cowboy watched this gathering fuss with rising interest. It mattered not to the tiny attacker that his moving target was multiple times his size. Nor did it move him that such hungry cats kill rodents and vermin with equal ease — and even those few birds that stupidly chance to fly within reach. After the fourth such shrieking onrush, the done in barn cat went hotfoot to the safety of the wooden structures Cowboy could see across the way.

"A'tween you and me, Dusty," Cowboy said, "that mock-a-bird don't fear nothin'. Don't back down none when he thinks he's right." The bird landed on the branch of a nearby, but smaller oak. His victory song continued non-stop for most of the next hour. During most of that while the wrangler managed a half-smile, remembering. In a whisper he said, "Pa always told us boys, 'courage is the hardest of the virtues.'" At that moment the wrangler wished he had more of it.

Cowboy soon watched the silhouette of a man move between house and barn. Whether relative or hired hand, he could not tell. Some minutes later, faint streaks of fluttering light began to dance along the one barn wall Cowboy could see through an open doorway. As it brightened, the big man knew a blacksmith's fire had been stoked.

Blowing to his face head-on, the light breeze carried the scent of budding mesquite and that of Acacia flowers. It brought with it the distinct sound of metal striking metal: irregular, varied strength of impact, and to Cowboy vaguely unsettling. The deep resonance of the clamor indicated that whatever object being struck was sizeable indeed.

When sun's rays first touched the topmost flange of blackened stove pipe, Cowboy saw a steady puff of smoke, the breakfast fire. At this distance, he imagined more than smelled the acrid char of wood. His stomach growled a bit as he recalled johnnycakes, eggs, and bacon his Ma would cook up most mornings. Sundays, birthdays, and special occasions saw the making of her specialty when she would happily announce, "Everything's better with biscuits."

Tempted as he now felt for a familiar hot meal to start this day, Cowboy chewed instead on bits of salted venison. He wanted to see more of the ranch's activity before bursting into their midst as either a surprise or dread. The wrangler did not recognize the tall contraption next to the old well. Its wooden beams stood clouded still in vague shadow. Where he sat under the oak, it favored a hangman's gallows.

From the under the porch on the side nearest the barn, two women emerged. The younger, her seeming red-brown hair swept into a bun, stood barely an inch or so taller than the other. A flowing gray apron covered the girl's plain farm dress. She carried a three-legged wooden stool upside down in one hand. The older woman, without mistake, Cowboy recognized as his Ma. The hair more gray, her walk now the slightest bit stiff, but the particular manner with which this wiry woman lugged the two-handled Stanley milk pail marked it definitely as her.

Cowboy drew breath at her familiar sight. The wrangler clenched one big hand around the oak's bark, tightening into a hard squeeze. That pounding in his chest he knew to be his heart, but it felt more like being walloped with a stout walking stick. He screwed eyes shut when they began to dampen, obscuring the woman from his vision for a long, long moment.

Next to the barn, a red roan mare and a gelding bay milled in the corral. Ears cocked on both as individually each one spotted the buckskin new to their grazing ground. In turn, they whinnied their greeting.

Hearing this overture, Dusty blew first through both nostrils then nickered back his loud reply.

At that sound, Cowboy's mother turned until her scrutiny beheld the lone figure and his mount together in the patch of oaks. She peered, but could not distinguish the man's identity. Ma said to the girl, "Would you just look at that." She nodded in the direction of the trees. "Must be the third drifter this month looking for some handout. He'll gladly settle for a hot meal." She turned back.

"At least this one looks to take good care of his horse. We'll feed him after chores." With that, the two women continued on to the barn.

Cowboy began to heave himself off the ground. "Dusty," he said in wistful tones, "recon I'll walk beside you over to the homeplace. Give them more time to see us coming, so as to better judge peaceful intent." The wrangler, instead, remained seated when he saw the man open the corral gate with saddle and bridle in hand. Even in the strengthened light, Cowboy was yet to say who he might be. But from the dispatch and ease with which he set and cinched the leathers on the bay, the man seemed no stranger to horses. He mounted, came through, and closed the corral gate in less time than Cowboy would have figured.

Still cross-legged under the oak, the big man watched the steady canter as approaching horse and rider closed the gap to his location. At a distance of about some fifty yards out, Cowboy smiled. He knew only one person to sit saddle in that particular manner. Neither did most men ride holding both reins by the left hand. When the horse got reined in, Cowboy stood.

Still seated on the gelding, the rider called out, "Reckon you're passing through. Where you hail from?"

"*No legos de aquí,*" Cowboy said in a deliberate flat tone. "Not far from here." He looked the other up and down. The face rounded more with maturity, no longer adolescent. The cleft in the chin, however, stayed the same. It took all the wrangler had not to bust into a wild fandango.

The man looked at Cowboy in turn for a long minute before fixing his attention on the buckskin. "That's a nice animal you ride, stranger." He nodded toward Dusty. "I guess you'll be wanting some grub before you head on your way."

Cowboy waited until their gaze met. Befuddlement that always comes before clear recognition flickered in the rider's eyes. To help the man out, the wrangler took a step closer toward the bay and removed the weathered Stetson. He stood so the man could see his full face in the sun. To him Cowboy said, "Older, taller, not so painfully thin. Still a good rider, and the first out of bed in the mornings. You always could talk the hinges off a gate. Ain't that right, Lucky?" Then Cowboy grinned.

Staring down into to the yet recognized tanned countenance, Lucky felt a shiver pass through his body. "Never seen that moustache before," he said. He looked deep into the wrangler's blue-grey eyes to be certain, swallowed once, and let go a breath. "Praise the Lord," he whispered. "*It is you!*"

***

From the very leaving of the oak patch, and without stopping for most of that short jaunt to the barn; Lucky all but crammed nine missing years of conversation into the length of the ride. His jabber answered some questions Cowboy held of family goings-on during his absence. Once inside the corral, Lucky stopped his bay alongside the buckskin. Seemingly now he drew only the second breath since recognizing his brother a half hour before.

"Ma is just going to jump over the moon," Lucky said. "She has waited for this day ever since you rode off on that skinny pinto." He grinned like a tinhorn holding aces in a game of draw. "You better have a darn good excuse to tell her, big brother," he said. "Deep in her heart she thought you was dead. But another part of her held out some meager hope." He leaned in close to Cowboy. "Every night, including this last one, she goes out on the porch. Don't matter the weather. She faces north, the direction she last saw you heading, and says a prayer." That news sobered Cowboy more than all that Riley Culpepper had told him.

The two dismounted. Without a word, they had removed tack and bridles from their mounts, freeing the horses to the expanse of the mesquite enclosure. Cowboy slid blanket and leathers over the split top rail of the fence, binding it securely. He angled back towards Lucky. "Let me put this off no longer," he said, drawing a deep breath. "I need to begin to make amends to her."

Both men stopped about three paces inside the barn. Behind them sunshine poured through the open large doorway, flooding the dirt floor and surroundings with unfiltered morning's light. In the stall centered on the far wall, a brown Durham cow chewed a jaw full of hay while the women tended to its milk-gorged udder. The younger, seated on the stool, slid a wooden bucket to the other. It brimmed with warm off-white liquid. Ma bent over the metal pale, her back to the doorway, ever so slowly draining raw milk into the dented container.

The younger woman noticed the pair of men as they stood motionless within an arm's length of where she sat. She stared at the stranger first, then at Lucky. His broad lopsided grin seemed out of place in the midst of restless cows, feed hay, and milk maid chores. He stood some two inches shorter, and a bit more narrow in the shoulder than the stranger, but shared the same sturdy cheekbones. "Is that..." she began before Lucky waved off the question by putting a single finger to his lips and a shake of his head.

"I fetched that drifter from the oak grove like you wanted," Lucky said. His eyes danced with laughter, confusing the girl even more.

Almost finished with her exacting task, his mother held her talk until the bucket emptied. "Good," she said, her back still to both of them. "Tell the man to wait and I'll cook him up enough to fill his belly."

Cowboy took two steps forward, removing his big hat for the second time that morning. The girl watched with eyes that grew larger as he approached. The big man said quietly, "Does that include some of your biscuits, Ma?" He braced himself to whatever came next.

For a moment nothing happened. Not a thing moved: not Ma, not the girl, not Lucky, nor Cowboy. Even the milk cow's constantly swishing tail stopped swatting at flies. With painful slowness Ma straightened from over the pail. The handle of the empty bucket held in one tiny hand, she turned toward the curious but not altogether unfamiliar voice. At first the sun's direct rays made her squint, standing as she had in comparative darkness. Cowboy took one step closer. His face alternated joy, pain, longing, and supplication in rapid order. His eyes locked onto hers. The milk bucket crashed to the dirt, rolling away slightly from her feet. Ma brought both hands to her mouth trying to cover the scream that came without warning. For such a slender woman, she filled the barn with ear-splitting noise.

Then she sobbed in more controlled tones, "My baby boy!" as Cowboy took her full in his arms. The two of them cried together for countless minutes. "As you always told us boys," he said, "there's nonesuch place as home."

Lucky grabbed his wife by the hand, lifting her off the milking stool. "Come on, Caroline, let's let them have the barn to themselves. They both need this." The two now-interlopers left quickly.

***

In the house's kitchen, Cowboy sat at the familiar long table. A filled coffee cup rested on it between his two big hands. He tried his best not to appear uncomfortable or lazy. Slow breathing helped. He had been instructed most lovingly by Ma to just sit where she could see him while she dealt with meal fixings.

The wrangler noticed his recently introduced sister-in-law peek up from the butter churn with every other stroke of the rod. Her hands rhythmically bumped the wooden splash guard on top. The look spread across her face bespoke more of indecision than curiosity.

On the fourth such glance Cowboy said to her, "What about me are you trying to determine, Caroline?"

"It's not you, really," she said. "It's my husband, your little brother. His description of you is nothing how I see you now." She paused to restate it better. "I mean the way he said you looked when you left home." She stopped again, adding: "Back then."

"Oh," Cowboy replied. A smile began at both corners of his mouth. "And, how was that exactly?"

"He never let on that you had such good looks," she said. Caroline shook her head at the same time to confirm her words. "The way I remember it, he said you were the kind of fellow that looked better in the dark." Red dotted both cheeks when she let that out.

Ma stopped kneading dough long enough to reply, "Lucky delights in turning a yarn just to see who will believe it." Cowboy nodded. "Why just before he went back to the blacksmith forge," she continued, "your big scamp of a husband asked me if I planned to make a batch of biscuits for each year my eldest here was prodigal." All three laughed.

Cowboy said lightly, "Appears Lucky might jes' care more for a stock of good biscuits than to actual seeing me again."

The big door at the front of the house opened without warning. An older man, slightly stooped, stepped in. The long black coat, his vest and trousers, together with the round-topped preacher's hat bore dust from his ride on the Atascosa roads. He stopped long enough to survey the scene around the table. The parson took in a deep sniff of the cooking aromas before focusing on the clump of dough in his wife's hands. Then he eyeballed the stranger. Cowboy stood to greet him.

The man approached, saying, "Biscuits in the making when Ma's birthday comes day after tomorrow. New horse in the paddock, and Lucky out in the barn grinning like a jackass eating briars." He stopped in front of Cowboy, almost height enough to look him eye-to-eye. "Can only mean one thing," he said, his usual sonorous voice no longer steady, "You've come home to us."

His words, "Praise God!" and Cowboy's murmured, "Pa," got muffled somewhere in each other's neck as the two bear-hugged in a telling grip. Both women let flow tears of joy where they stood; to them the sight too precious. Stepping back finally from the embrace, Pa took an appraising look at his son. He grabbed the offered hand to pump over and over again. "First tell us you'll stay, then assure us you paid real money for that big buckskin outside. After that you can speak of your journey."

Cowboy could only nod, his voice lost for now. He knew it would take minutes, and a bit more of Ma's hot coffee to recover.

Pa sat opposite him at the table. He tossed his hat in a nearby chair. From a back pocket he took a kerchief to rub his nose before accepting the steaming cup Ma handed him. Seeing the sheer exhaustion in the parson's face, she asked, "How was the all-night vigil at Widow Jenkin's house?"

The man raised his eyes from the cup. "Martha's fever broke much, much sooner than the Doc expected. Said he'd never seen anything like it. Expects her to live." He spooned sugar into the coffee, tasted it, and smiled his approval. "I thought that most providentially strange, until I saw you." Pa nodded to Cowboy. "I know now that God meant me to hurry home." He placed his big hand on that of Cowboy's. "Two miracles in the space of one morning. I am doubly blessed."

***

Cowboy could not imagine doing this belabored task on any August afternoon. Rhythmic creaking of the thick wooden handle, the accompanying burst of hissing air, followed apace by its loud intake again created the only sound within the open barn. The big man tugged a blacksmith's bellows without stopping. Broken ember chunks, the remains of fired mesquite glowed intense orangey-red. An almost invisible flame flickered along their top. The small forge's heat reddened the wrangler's face. His chest bare beneath the leather apron, his back and neck all dripped sweat.

"You've got to make it hotter this time," Lucky shouted, "or the weld will just break again." The smaller man struggled to hold the two jagged pieces of broken lift rod in the fire at the proper angle. Balancing one on each shoulder, he held the tips of both centered in the brightest glow.

Cowboy redoubled his effort, pumping faster, and watching the color slowly become almost white. After a quarter hour, the rod tips radiated a similar hue.

"Now," Lucky yelled. He passed off one rod to his brother as they both hurried to the anvil horn where the two ends, already disturbed and beaten into scarfing angles, met to form one continuous metal shaft. Lucky struck at this new seam over and again. He rotated the metal, banging away again until the lift rod lost its heat.

Cowboy watched his brother's eyes to gauge the other's satisfaction with the work. First a slight nod, then another. Lucky grinned but did not address the metal at their knees. "I'll wager you rather be in this barn mastering smithy chores, than sitting around the kitchen playing mama's boy to a woman that won't seem to let you out of her sight again."

The big man looked over one shoulder before nodding his agreement.

"Best we let this weld cool of its own," Lucky said. "No water this time. I'll take the hammer to it in the morning, strike the seam and see if she'll hold this time." He shook his head, experiencing some doubt.

Cowboy struggled to unknot the tangled apron strings behind his back. His eye caught sight of the makeshift contrivance in the corner. What at one time must have been a buggy's wheel, now went without the steel rim and the curved wooden felloes. Every extended spoke now sported thin, hand-hewn oaken staves; each affixed to the wheel hub by a stout rivet. Cowboy speculated that the metal rod protruding where the axel arm should be meant this to be a clumsy attempt at a windmill wheel. He looked at Lucky, now putting away the tongs and hammer. But the wrangler said nothing.

Both men grabbed up belongings, walked the short way to the well's pump, and doused themselves clean with buckets of clear water.

As they dried and donned shirts and hats once more, a clatter could be heard from inside the kitchen nearby. "Uh-oh, big brother," Lucky said with a laugh. "Best we *vamonos toda prisa* before the women put us to doing jobs we're no good at." He snapped a suspender over one shoulder, all but running to saddle the bay. "Got to go check the sluice on the back property line,' he said as he mounted up. "River in the north county up on its banks already. Francisco Perez and San Miguel Creeks show they're beginning to rise." He nodded. "Must be raining something fierce way up in the hill country."

Cowboy shot him a query with raised eyebrows, to which the younger brother replied, "Come to think on it, you don't know about the sluice." He shrugged, searching his mind for when this was built. "We fill this big stock pond each year with runoff from spring rains. Mostly it's enough water to last when the creek winds down to a trickle. Let's us raise other than longhorn cattle, which don't seem to need regular water."

Cowboy rode his big horse in silence, as he usually did on the trail. He felt no need at that moment to speak about cattle, family, or travels to Lucky. He calculated it a slim chance to get a word in while his brother rambled on about the construction detail of the narrow channel run between the creek and the pond.

The wrangler judged that Lucky sold a story short for once. Setting his eye upon the hand-dug gully carrying water to a meandering reservoir, Cowboy knew this had been a massive undertaking. He said, "I can remember there being a shallow *barranco* right about here. That ravine wadn't no more than hip deep."

"That's right," Lucky said. "And fifty yards wide. Used to open out into those mesquite breaks yonder." He pointed southeast to open land. So's we took what's dug up making the sluice and dammed the far end." His unexpected laugh caught Cowboy unawares. "That bank did not hold the first year, and we lost most of the water. Now it works just fine."

Cowboy dismounted the buckskin to take a closer look at the water moving across the spillway. It moved at a slow but steady stream through the sluice before rippling down the bank. The collected pool already covered the tank's bottom all the distance to the far embankment. The wrangler judged it would fill in about a week's time.

His attention shifted when he felt Dusty jerk at the reins Cowboy held in his hand. He focused on the rider approaching through the brush. From the pony's relaxed gait, it appeared to be a friendly visit by someone no stranger to the ranch. "Who might that be?" Cowboy asked. "He sets a saddle well," nodding his approval, "For sure knows how to ride a horse."

That drew a grin from Lucky, but no words. He waited further exposition, but got none. His brother seemed too engaged in watching the rider's effortless skill. "Oh, that would be Lee McAllister," he said. "Inherited the old Potter Ranch next door when the aunt and uncle died childless."

The rider topped the slight rise, reined in the chestnut pony, and glanced at both men with no particular hurry. "Afternoon, pard," Lee said to Lucky in firm tones, but turned to look straight at Cowboy. From underneath the rider's dark felt hat, green eyes narrowed. Hair the color of just-cut hay jutted from the brim long enough to cover both ears and a bit of cheek. Cowboy judged it likely grew past the rear neckband of the wrinkled wool shirt.

A red wind rag wrapped twice around the neck. Its fancy knot secured the bandana in place, one long end loosely draped over the right shoulder while the other hung down to cover the top button of the open collar.

"Who's your friend there?" Lee asked. Green eyes moved up and down, assessing the big man before any identity given.

Lucky flashed an impish grin. "Oh, that's my eldest brother," he said. The one I been telling you about; gone missing all this time."

Cowboy stared back in return. Something about this trim cowpoke with chaps hanging down to boot heels, and an almost new lariat tied to the saddle did not square in his mind. Not until the head turned and he could see full profile.

"You the one went off to see the elephant?" Lee asked Cowboy directly. The voice came softer this time, still full of interest.

"Yes, ma'am," the wrangler answered. He realized the rider now holding his gaze to be a woman

"So, how was it?" she asked, crossed forearms over her saddle horn, and waited the telling of his tale.

***

As ranch rides go, Cowboy counted the amble home from the stock pond enjoyable: a mild afternoon with the promise of warming, the company of two good riders on two good horses, and the sheer joy Dusty seemed to show knowing this range might be a place to settle. They loped three abreast through the scrub and mesquite thickets. Lee rode between and slightly in front of the two brothers; turning her head as she conversed with Lucky, turning back as she just watched Cowboy ride.

He said little more than "yes" or "no" when addressed with questions, concentrating more on the talk between Lucky and the young woman. By the time this trio reached the homestead, the wrangler learned that Lee had owned and worked the Potter Ranch for no more than a year, mostly by herself. Her uncle's two ranch hands left soon after the funeral, themselves too old to be much help any longer. Lucky helped out in their stead as best he could. This undaunted woman who sat a horse with such ease also took spiritual counsel from the two men's father, and even from their brother, Marcus, whenever that young parson came to Atascosa. Cowboy smiled almost without showing it. Lee McAllister was a hard working, God fearing woman. She also had need of an experienced ranch hand.

Two buggies sat beside the house as they approached. One jacketed completely in dust, the other newer with an almost pristine appearance. The carriage horses rested without motion, except for the occasional fly swat.

"Now *everyone* is here," Lucky said. His good cheer sounded as genuine as it did heartfelt. He slid off the bay and tied leathers, not waiting for his companions. He hurried through the front door. From within, merry voices talking one over the other, plus the constant yelp of children's laughter could be heard.

Cowboy let Lee precede him into the room. At his entry, all conversation stopped. Even the three young children held their noise to stare up at the tall stranger. A single man rose. Slightly shorter than Lucky, but eighteen months his senior, Marcus walked without hesitation to his older brother. He threw his arms around him in a tight clench, but said not a word. "I thought about you many times on the trail, *hermano*," Cowboy said at last.

In return, the spirited preacher from Uvalde replied, "In my daily prayers, I asked for this day to come." He showed the small beginnings of a smile. "Now all of us are blessed." They hugged again with even greater warmth. Ma and Caroline cried quietly into their aprons.

Stepping back from that warm embrace, Cowboy looked into the eyes of a near stranger, the kid brother they affectionately all called "little Johnny". The man standing before the wrangler, no longer a tow-headed urchin of twelve, stood almost to Cowboy's own height. Johnny's strapping torso gave him the clear weight advantage over the older brother. He grabbed Cowboy's extended hand with such a crushing grip that the eldest brother immediately wondered what Ma had been feeding the boy all this time.

Johnny said to him, "You probably don't remember me much on account I was so young when you left. But do know that I was the one that missed you the most." His longing look searched Cowboy's face. "I always looked up to you. You did everything better, stronger, and smarter than the rest of us."

Johnny shifted from one big foot to the other until Cowboy pulled him, too, into an embrace. It crossed the wrangler's mind what misjudgment this hug might be when his wind got near choked out of him by a squeeze worthy of the monster bear that day at the cave.

"Let him go, you big galoot. It's my turn." The man got elbowed aside by a most pregnant mother-to-be. Cowboy did not recall the little lady's voice all at once, but he did know the eyes on top of that smile. She'd flashed them at him often enough as an irrepressible little tomboy: Alice, Riley Culpepper's little sister. She stepped in to clinch arms around his waist for a brief but warm hug. "Truth is," she said, "none of us thought we'd see you alive again. Word actually came of your unfortunate demise."

At that, Cowboy laughed. He turned to look at the only unfamiliar person in the room. This woman sat at the kitchen table next to his Ma. With her free arm, she clutched a pair of lookalike young boys. In her lap their little sister cuddled. Marcus did the honors, 'This is my wife, Lydia, the twins, Gideon and Nathanael, and our daughter, Hannah."

The woman smiled the warm greeting of a dedicated preacher's wife. "We've brought a cake for your mother's birthday, but she insists that we dedicate it instead to celebrate your return." Lydia patted Ma's forearm before nodding to a spot across the room. "Also, Alice has made some of her wonderful punch." She smiled again as though she'd known Cowboy all her life. "We'll have that after supper. I'm glad you could join us here today."

Cowboy said his thanks and greeting. He took her hand briefly, but his curiosity about Lee's role in all of this stole most of his attention. That query got somewhat addressed when his Ma stepped over to the only female at this gathering fitted out in riding duds. She took the young woman by the elbow to lead her nearly face-to-face with her eldest son. "I see that you've already met our Leanora here," his mother said to him.

"Yes," Cowboy responded in a soft baritone. "It's a lovely name."

Two circles of red grew on very tanned cheeks. The new owner of Potter's Ranch wished to be anywhere else in the world that moment; just not in this suddenly crowded room. Redness deepened when she heard Cowboy choke back his laughter. Yet, she relaxed a bit when she saw the seeds of gentleness begin to flicker in his eyes.

***

"If I can reach it with the palm of my hand, then it's too short to be a windmill." Johnny proved his point to Lucky by setting his empty punch glass atop the wooden cross piece without even needing to stand on tiptoes. Marcus and Pa nodded as Lucky muttered incoherence and kicked dirt with his boot. "You should have made it taller," the youngest brother went on. "But so far it hasn't blown over yet. And I believe you told Ma it's pumped maybe ten gallons in the six months since you planted it." At that remark a round of belly laughs burst out from everyone — everyone except Cowboy.

"It just needs more help is all," the wrangler said evenly.

"Then let us pray he gets it soon," Marcus said with mirth. "Or else he'll spend even more time trying to piece together that hand-me-down metal into a working machine."

Lucky startled the others when he jerked himself around to square off with them, leaning shoulders forward, fists raised chest-high. Cowboy judged that dark look on his face meant Lucky had determined to brawl. The younger brother stared each of the siblings in the eye. Studiously, he avoided Pa's stern look.

Lucky spit out, "Go ahead, it's easy for you to laugh. I'm the one bounden to work this hardscrabble ranch." His body shook with pent up feelings. "Just me, Caroline, and Ma. Pa when he don't have no parson chores. I'm not the one what caught the eye of the banker's daughter and

110

got me a job in town. And I didn't get the Gospel call as a boy and take up Devil chasing in Uvalde." Then he turned to Cowboy standing closest to him. "We're getting by, but just barely. Nothing left over to get us anything like a real windmill." He breathed in labored gasps before his voice trailed off with, "These days it's hard to sell cattle to just about anyone." The glare from his focused stare all but carried heat to Cowboy's face.

"We'll have no more of that talk," Pa began to admonish his next-to-youngest.

Cowboy waived his father off with a big hand. He stepped up close to his querulous brother. To him he said, "Is this about the windmill, or is something on your mind you mean to say to me direct?"

Lucky raised himself up, trying to stretch to the same height as Cowboy. When he realized that would never happen, he let out a sigh and took a half-step back. "You leaving in such a hurry," he said, "left us all flat-footed. And, you've been gone so long." Hands spread in front of his chest, wide enough to pass his shoulders. "Now you're back again. It caught us all flat-footed once more." He looked around for affirmation, but found none. "Well, me anyway," he said. Arms fell to his sides as his anger sank into dismay. In a plaintive voice now tinged with hurt, Lucky said, "It ain't right you just showing up out of nowhere and expecting to take over the ranch just 'cause you're the oldest."

For a second, no sound could be heard except for the women conversing on the porch. Yet at that instant Cowboy's face lit up with gut-felt relief. He grinned. His new comfort came from the realization that he had now completed the circle of his journey. It began with a fistfight and now might finish with another. Of ending that way, he saw no need. The wrangler asked, "That what got you vexed up like a young bull at the first sign of spring? Me pulling this place out from under you? Until I spoke with Riley Culpepper last week in Schulenburg, I didn't know there even was a ranch to come home to." He laughed at his own misconception.

"What?!" came almost simultaneously from all three younger brothers. Pa just nodded at this curiosity, as if he had seen it coming all along.

Cowboy ignored their question to say, "I already told Ma and Pa here, I ain't going nowhere as long as I can spend what time we got left being with them. You worked the ranch all this while, it's yours to run." He nodded to himself first, then to Lucky. "I will help out best I can where's it you need me, but only as *segundo* to you." Cowboy's big grin returned. He stepped up to Lucky with a big hand extended. "Unless you go off and do somethin' plum locoed, like try and steal a biscuit off my breakfast plate." Cowboy turned to the others with a wink. "A kid brother will do that to a fella."

This time Lucky lead the laughter as he pumped the hand offered. His eyes took on a guarded look of merriment. "And this?" he nodded, indicating the gallows-like wooden structure.

"Oh, I think I might could help you a bit more with that," Cowboy said.

Pa indicated for his sons to gather close. They did so without hesitation, evidencing years of practice. "The parable of the prodigal son," he said, "in the Book of Luke has no ending. Jesus just stopped talking where He did. To this day it is unclear what exactly the older brother did in the days that followed." The preacher put one hand on Lucky. "In our case, a younger brother worked the fields while the older brother went away." He then set the other hand on Cowboy. "This brother here certainly did not take family riches with him to squander in far off places. From what I can tell, his was a journey of the spirit. Now he has returned. No fatted calf. Merely a birthday cake shared with his mother." The preacher stood back, indicating all of them with a sweeping hand. "As in the parable, each of you has got to decide, 'how will I act now toward my returning brother?'" He paused, before adding, "Both today and in the days to come." They answered his challenge by slapping Cowboy playfully, but somewhat roughly on the back and shoulders.

Marcus and Johnny soon joined their Pa on the walk back to the house. Without speaking, they knew enough to leave Lucky with Cowboy by themselves to work out any remaining misgivings.

To Cowboy's questioning look, Lucky responded, "I didn't mean to have such a case of the grouch just now." For a moment he studied his boot leathers. "It's a kick in the gut when you work calluses on your fingers month-in-and-month-out, got no money for any trivials, and your best efforts to build something needed draw only scorn." Still looking down he reached to pull something from a back pocket. "When I read this and then got poked fun at I saw everything slipping away. Truth is, I was happy as all get out when you first rode up. Even liked working together in the barn. But as I thought on it more, I got scared." Lucky looked up. "For a moment, it seemed like you came home to rescue your little brother just like you always did. The white knight once more." He handed the telegram to Cowboy. Lucky said, "The look in your eyes just now tells me I got it all wrong. I apologize. You mean this as a gift to all of us with only sincerity in your heart."

Cowboy read aloud, "Flint & Walling Model 12 Star windmill freighted to you by San Antonio Machine & Supply Company. Expect next ten days. Gift from the returning wanderer. Regards, Riley Culpepper, Esq."

Looking up from the page, Cowboy said, "It's a long tale for another time. Short ways, I'll just say it's honest bought. All that time on the trail with not much to spend wages on if you don't give in to temptations of the flesh."

Lucky looked up to the pale blue eyes of his older brother. "I don't give a good fried apple where the money came from," he said. His face mellowed into a soft smile. "I'll just say thanks and be grateful."

Cowboy threw one arm around Lucky's neck. They walked to join the others on the porch.

***

In a mood of idleness after the breakfast meal, Cowboy watched the bent pewter spoon continuously push coffee into a swirl as he stirred it round the cup and around again. The porcelain clutched in one palm felt almost hot to the touch; comforting on this cool morning. Steam wet his face and eyebrows as he sat bent over the table taking in fresh aroma. His own dented container that he drank from daily on the trail lay still hidden in the leathers of his saddlebag now pegged up in the barn. Home life, he thought to himself, with all it promised of hard work, would be a pure pleasure getting used to.

Pa set the brass cartridge back onto the table's top with a clang. That noise broke the spell of Cowboy's silent reverie. Pa said, "You say that's a .50 caliber rifle?" The Big Fifty leaned against an empty chair. Cowboy nodded, taking pleasure from his father's obvious delight in the examination of the Sharps buffalo gun; a gift of the prodigal's journey from his oldest son. With some amazement, the parson picked up the bullet once more to place it across his palm as if to demonstrate. From tip of the rounded lead to the base of the flattened rim, the cartridge stretched the entire width of the man's broad hand. With a jesting grin, but mock-serious tones, Pa announced, "Jackalopes of south Texas beware. Now I have fierce new armament, and shall fear thee no longer. Best you hide when you see me approach." He looked at Cowboy across the table with dead-set eyes.

"They squirrel away now already, don't they?" Cowboy asked.

"True," Pa said. "But now I shall know the reason why."

They both laughed at his jest.

Ma laughed, too, as she stepped up with the offer of more hot coffee from the stove. She said nothing. As her son's eyes met hers, she merely touched the brooch pinned to her blouse with extended fingertips. Her smile made the entirety of his heart begin to feel warm as the coffee in his grip. "It looks good on you, Ma," he said, after choking back a small lump forming at the front of his throat.

"Tell me that story again," she requested, set the big pot on the table, and seated herself to listen.

Cowboy was quick to indulge her. A carved alabaster likeness of an unknown but undoubtedly beautiful woman held fast to the translucent seashell back piece. This cameo jewelry Ma now wore evidenced superb and patient craftsmanship. He said, "The last time I chanced to visit my old saddle pal Ray and his pretty wife Esmeralda in Cowtown, she pressed me to buy you a grand keepsake from my travels to give you when I finally reached Atascosa again." He thought of that afternoon with sweet recall. "I guess it's always easy for a person to spend someone else's money, but I didn't mind." He looked at the brooch once more. "She took me to this fancy store on the good side of town. Folks there knew her, so the trade seemed fair." Cowboy tapped a place on the side of his chest beneath the arm where his coat would have touched. "Didn't dwell on it at the time, but seems I always carried it in the pocket here, next to my heart." Her smile swelled from mere fondness to that of a mother's unbounded love.

Captured still by her affection she asked, "You are going to help out Leanora today, are you not?"

"Yes, ma'am," Cowboy said. "Lucky is sending me there in his place. Reckon he'll be doing that steady once the windmill parts arrive."

"She's a fine woman, don't you think?" Ma asked. She did not even begin to hide the twinkle now in her eye. Pa looked on as if this were to be expected, and something in which he certainly should not meddle.

"Yes, ma'am," her son said again. "I know she can ride. Today I'll see how she sets with cattle." His twinkle began to match her own.

***

How she set with cattle, Cowboy could not easily determine at this distance. He seemed of two minds, sitting on Dusty some quarter-mile back-trailed, watching. On one hand, Lee worked the stock with an uneasy resolve. Not nearly as effortless as Lucky, she herded the beeves with a nonetheless resolute determination. On the other hand, he could tell that more days dogging the herefords on this ranch would have her as his brother's equal.

Two pair of young white-face split off from the milling beeves, catching Lee on the far side. To chase them meant giving up control of the herd she now pushed single-handed toward the watering tank. Her eyes betrayed evil thoughts toward these four delinquents, but her concentration remained with the other cattle. Lee did not see Cowboy until he cantered Dusty to cut the strays off from the open land they now trotted towards. Their leader dashed at a quick right angle to the horse and rider as those two approached the strays head-on. Dusty lunged in front of the yearling, cutting off his advance. The hereford wheeled an opposite direction to race past the horse that way. Again the buckskin cut off his advance. Cowboy did little more than touch Dusty's sides with one knee or the other, to let the big horse know which way to anticipate.

After a minute-and-a-half of such twists and false turns, the hereford stopped, looked at the horse and rider blocking his path, and gave up the effort by turning back the way he had come with his followers in tow. Five more minutes and the four were back with the herd.

"Morning," Cowboy said with all due pleasantry. A greeting Lee returned in kind.

She wondered aloud, "Do all the brothers handle cattle as well as you and Lucky?"

"Been known to," he said with a grin, "Not likely so much anymore. Marcus and Johnny got else on their minds."

"And you're better at it than the other three, I'd say," Lee said, watching for his reaction.

Cowboy replied nothing to that, or to the appraising look she covered him with for a long moment. "If you're looking for a top hand to help you mind your ranch," he said, "I'd be obliged if you'd give me some consideration. Lucky could use me some, but really not all that much. He has a good handle on it."

Lee liked his direct but understated approach. "What did you have in mind?" she asked.

"I figure it's easier on all of us to run your stock and ours as one big herd. We got no fences and share the water now as it is," he said. "Got this new pal up north of Cowtown name of Calvin Quinn; married to a good Christian woman. She's gone and adopted me like some big brother or uncle." Cowboy shifted in the saddle to face Lee more directly. "They run a feedlot together that sells beef back east. Cal says he'll buy all the good cattle I'll bring him." He watched Lee take all this in with calm consideration.

After a moment's thought, Lee said, "Sure. I figure that's worth a try." She smiled at this man she'd taken an instant liking to. "I'll take you on. We'll work out the particulars with Lucky, but I can see this turning into something good." After a moment more she added, "You have a lot more cattle experience than me. I'll watch and learn."

"Yes ma'am," Cowboy said the third time that morning. "But you're the boss."

Lee laughed at the irony of that. She followed Cowboy and Dusty as he began to push the cattle to water. "One thing I'd like to ask, if it's not too personal," she said. "Lucky claims they called the four of you the Gospel Brothers. He never explained the reason." Lee hesitated. "Would you mind telling me why?"

Cowboy grinned at that old nickname. "I saw you flinch when Ma called you Leonora. You prefer to go by Lee. We have that in common." He drew Dusty up next to her mount. "Folks call me Eden, but even that's not the exact name. I was born Mathew Edenfield DeWitt."

Lee looked at him not fully understanding this as an answer to her question.

He continued, "Pa is a powerful man of God. He names us boys Mathew, Mark, Luke, and John. Me, Marcus, Lucky, and little Johnny—the Gospel Brothers. Any wonder we changed our names?"

Lee let this sink in a bit. Then she smiled with a budding new affection. She spurred her horse, calling over a shoulder, "Come on. We got cattle to chase, Eden."

He bobbed a head in agreement, stirring his own mount.

Turning their horses toward the now moving herd, they loped the trail at an easy pace.

Their journey together had just begun.

Nonesuch
Study Questions

1. As Pa said, each person in the family had a choice of how he would act toward his brothers, like in the parable of the prodigal son. Do you have more trouble showing love toward people like Cowboy or people like Lucky? How does knowing Jesus loves you allow you to show love to others?

2. Cowboy brought gifts for his family on his return that reminded him of specific stories of God's protection and guidance on his journey. What are some of your memories of God's goodness to you on your journey?

3. Cowboy was concerned about his parents' reaction when he came home, but Ma and Pa accepted him immediately. How is their thrill at Cowboy returning like God's desire for each of us to come back to him? What do you need to do to come home to God?

Epilogue

Epilogue

125

"I'll go home to my parents, confess what I've done,
And I'll ask them to pardon their prodigal son,
And if they caress me as oft times before,
Then I never will play the Wild Rover no more."

*** The Wild Rover***
Traditional Irish Folksong
Author Unknown

Call to Action

Dear Lord Jesus,

I know that I am a sinner,
and I ask for Your forgiveness.

I believe You died for my sins
and rose from the dead.

I turn from my sins and invite
You to come into my life.

I want to trust and follow
You as my Lord and Savior.

In Your Name.
Amen

Dusty's Song

I am an old range rider,
I follow the cattle trail—
Just me and my *caballo*,
Our journey's quite the tale.

I still rope and wrangle,
Can toss a steer with ease,
I spur my big horse Dusty—
To take me where I please.

About Cowboy Church

Cowboy churches are local Christian churches within the cowboy culture that are distinctively Western heritage in character. A typical cowboy church may meet in a rural setting in a barn, metal building, arena, sale barn, or old western building; have its own rodeo arena, and a country gospel band.

Baptisms are generally done in a stock tank. The sermons are usually short and simple, in order to be better understood by the parishioners. Some cowboy churches have covered arenas where rodeo events such as bull riding, team roping, ranch sorting, team penning and equestrian events are held on weeknights.

Many cowboy churches have existed throughout the western states for the past forty or fifty years, however just in the past fifteen or so years has there been an explosion of growth within the "movement".

Prior to 1980 there were no less than 5 cowboy churches in Texas, now the number exceeds 200, and there are an estimated 750 nationwide. There has been no definitive group that established the movement; rather it seems to have had a spontaneous beginning in diverse areas of the country at nearly the same time.

Some of these cowboy churches are an outgrowth of ministries to professional rodeo or team roping events, while the roots of many can be traced back to ministry events associated with ranch rodeos, ranch horse competitions, chuck wagon cooking competitions, cowboy poetry gatherings and other "cowboy culture" events.

Introducing
Team Dusty

About the Author

T. W. Lawrence is a native Texan. Born at the edge of the Hill Country near San Antonio, his father was a successful veterinarian and his mother taught in the nearby junior high school.

Words — their meanings and origins — were always a topic of family conversation as T. W. grew up. Writing was a natural offshoot of his active imagination and capacity for poetic observations.

His long-time writing career has produced a portfolio that includes more than forty published articles, six professional course manuals, the short story anthology *Take Me To Texas*, and the novels, *Texas Cool Million* and *Tracks of the Sandman*.

He is a member of Christian Writers Guild, American Christian Fiction Writers, Western Writers of America, and Writers' League of Texas.

Bryan Tyson

Deacon, Johnson Ferry Baptist Church

Bryan is one of those people who enjoys to read and to teach others. He has studied theological topics for years and leads Sunday School classes on topics ranging from systematic theology to church history. Bryan also travels internationally as a missionary to teach pastors on theological topics.

He lives in Marietta, Georgia, with his wife and three daughters. When he's not buried in a book, teaching, or chasing his young daughters through the house, Bryan is a lawyer and heads up the public defender system for the state of Georgia.

Bryan earned his *juris doctor* from the Oak Brook College of Law.

His hope is to one day become a real cowboy.

Moby

Moby in the Morning

Moby's alarm has been going off every weekday morning at 3:30 for the past 40 years and he loves it. It means he will soon be in front of the microphone doing what he does best—entertaining the thousands of members of his radio family across this great country.

Moby started his radio career at the age of 15 in Crossville, Tenn., his hometown and the place he got the nickname, Moby. Although he had other career plans, he was hooked. He enrolled in college with the idea of becoming a high school band director, but soon gave it up to pursue his dream of a radio career. From Nashville to Houston and Dallas to Atlanta, he's been an early-morning fixture for fans across the South.

For Moby, it's always been and will always be about the music, the listeners, and the country we ALL love.

It's that passion for what he does and the deep understanding of who his listeners are that have made him a proud member of the Country Radio Hall of Fame. He is also the five-time winner of Billboard's Major Market Country Morning Show of the Year and two-time nominee for the Major Market Morning Show of the Year by the CMA. He has also been honored as Academy of Country Music's Major Market DJ of the Year.

Moby shares his life with his third and favorite wife yet, Mary Beth, (she's told him that IF there's a fourth wife, it had better be a nurse with money) and his only female child, 10 year old daughter Grace, who can never date! They reside just outside of Atlanta, GA.

To connect with Moby, visit
www.mobyinthemorning.com

Sandy Weaver Carman

CEO, Voicework on Demand

Sandy Weaver Carman is the driving force behind Voicework on Demand, Inc., an audio production company specializing in audio book and audio learning production. Sandy spent her career on the radio, working in Atlanta, Washington DC, Boston and Columbus, GA. It was during her radio career that she fell in love with audio production, and in 2008, she decided to start a company. As a voice talent and audio editor, Sandy works with writers, coaches, trainers and speakers, helping them to create audio programs from their books, webinars and keynotes. Whether working with audio they provide or starting from scratch and talking their words, Sandy develops products for her clients that provide a revenue river – income from work they've already done.

As a writer, Sandy has article publishing credits going back to her teens, and she finally buckled down and wrote an entire book. "The Original MBA— Succeed in Business Using Mom's Best Advice" is a story-filled book of life lessons that help students, new hires and job-changers get a leg up in their careers. She's also written "Create a Revenue River," an e-book designed to help those who wish to create their own audio products. She's a sought-after speaker, wowing audiences with useable information packaged inside fun stories.

In her personal life, Sandy is married to Bob Carman, a long-time employee at IBM. He golfs, she tries, but her favorite sport is anything that can include their dogs. They have two Siberian Huskies, and Sandy is not just a competitor in conformation, obedience, agility and pack-hiking, she's a licensed AKC judge. Sandy is the Education Coordinator for the Siberian Husky Club of America and is a budding runner and tri-athlete. They live just outside of Atlanta, GA.

To connect with Sandy, visit
http://about.me/SandyWeaverCarman

Vanessa Lowry

Graphic Designer, Marketing Consultant, Radio Host

In addition to designing the covers for T.W. Lawrence's print and audio books, Vanessa creates marketing materials such as business cards, posters, and more.

Wearing her radio host hat, Vanessa interviewed T.W. on Write Here, Write Now and Art as Worship. Links to these show archives are available on:

www.Connect4Leverage.com.

T.W. talks about how Project Dusty evolved on Write Here, Write Now. After clicking on the page link for Write Here, Write Now Radio, scroll down to "Print and Audio…Leveraging Content."

On Art as Worship, T.W. discusses how creating the Dusty series transformed his own faith journey and continues to guide his spiritual path. Click the Art as Worship Radio link and find Walter (T.W.) Lawrence in the list of artists to access the 30-minute discussion.

Vanessa says, "I am grateful to be a member of Team Dusty and help T.W. bring his design and marketing ideas to life. I love the joy of collaborating with him."

Find out more about Vanessa and
the services she provides authors at
www.Connect4Leverage.com

Michael Belk

Journeys with the Messiah

Michael Belk's photography has appeared in Vogue, GQ and Vanity Fair for clients that include Nautica, J.Crew and others. A self-taught photographer, his career began in the fashion industry - first in retail, and then as a sales executive for a prestigious men's clothing line in the 60s and 70s. Then, photography snagged his soul.

Combining his gift for photography with a natural sense for sales and marketing, Michael began creating print collateral and, eventually, advertising campaigns throughout the clothing industry. With his unique style and quality of products, his business and his reputation grew. He has been the man behind the camera, the creative director and the account executive for his own boutique agency.

After 30 successful years, Michael sensed that God had even greater plans for him and he began to pursue an idea that he believes God put on his heart. In 2008, he put his career on hold to begin work on a collection of fine art photographs that would depict messages of Jesus—showing His relevance in our modern world. The project, Journeys with the Messiah, was first published in late 2009 and has since received accolades from around the world as God visually connect hearts to His Son.

The images have been produced as limited-edition fine art pieces, a coffee table book, behind the scenes DVD, posters and more. Michael travels to churches and other organizations to present the story of "his journey

with the Messiah" in an exciting audio/visual presentation.
An exhibit, film and more images are planned.

Explore the images at
www.JourneyswiththeMessiah.org

Coming Soon

From

T.W. Lawrence

Brewster and Bailey:
Teenage Buckaroos

(2016)

Dusty and the Cowboy

Audiobooks

Downloads:

Audible.com
iTunes

CDs:

Amazon

eBooks

Kindle
Nook
iTunes

Contact Information

www.facebook.com/DustyAndTheCowboy

DustyAndTheCowboy@gmail.com

www.DustyAndTheCowboy.com

www.ingramcontent.com/pod-product-compliance
Lightning Source LLC
Chambersburg PA
CBHW020616120726
47905CB00003B/825